*Joe Lan*

BOOK 1

# ISLAND LIES

Joe Langley: Island Lies
By Ronnie Ashmore

Published by Creative Texts Publishers, LLC
PO Box 50
Barto, PA 19504
www.creativetexts.com

ISBN: 978-1-64738-104-2

*Joe Langley*

BOOK 1

# ISLAND LIES

by

RONNIE ASHMORE

*For My Mom, gone since 2015, and there is so much she never got to see. She would be proud of the books I have written and would be asking when the next one is coming out. She was the first person to read what I considered masterpieces when I was a teenager. She never criticized my effort. She was a good mom, and I hope I made her proud.*

# Contents

# 1

I have always been a dreamer, much to the chagrin of my family and friends, it seems. I have always wanted to travel to distant lands, visit other cities, and meet other people my whole life. I would be hard-pressed to remember a time when I didn't wish to be somewhere else, doing something else. But I had never been out of my home state.

My whole life, it seemed, was lived in a rush to get somewhere other than where I found myself at the time. That was how I was feeling now, like I wanted to be somewhere else.

I was sitting at the bar nursing my seventh or maybe eighth scotch of the night while thinking about my life to this point. It was something I did routinely, both drink and brood, most every night, in fact.

I had been successful, the way most people would define that word, anyway. I had gone to law school and landed a job in a big firm but didn't find joy in that. Went to the police academy. Policing did not pay what I thought I should be making. I was unemployed for a while, that didn't pay well either.

But for the past ten years, I have been working as a private investigator. I got my private investigator license and opened my own business, Joseph V. Langley and Associates. It had a fancy sound to the title, even though there were no associates, and never had been. At first, business started off booming, now not so much.

Divorce took most of my money and any retirement I had. Jenny, that is my ex-wife's name. That's what she wanted to be called, not Jennifer like her parents had named her. Anyway, she and I rarely spoke. When we did, it was always in hostile tones that ended in an argument. Luckily, we had no kids to put through that grist mill.

I ordered another scotch, my eighth, or ninth, I couldn't recall.

I watched my favorite bartender work. Her name is Amanda. I don't know her last name. I knew nothing about her away from this bar. She was a damn pretty woman. I enjoyed watching her work. She had long, thick, black hair. She wore it down tonight. It framed her face, adding to the smile she often gave to customers. Tonight, she was wearing a short black skirt. Her legs moved her gracefully around the back of the bar as she made drinks. One perk of coming here was just to be near her, which was good enough for me. I sipped my drink.

This was how I spent most evenings. Getting blitzed to the point that I might not remember anything in the morning, like, for instance, how I got home.

A stranger was sitting next to me. I was not aware of when she had sat down. One minute I was alone at the edge of the bar, the next she was looking right at me.

She was pretty, I would give her that. Her brown hair in a ponytail, a few errant strands falling over her face. The make-up hid a few wrinkles. I placed her age in the late thirties. She was watching me stare at her. I turned my gaze away.

"I need to hire you, I think," she said, sipping her own drink.

"Me?" I laughed softly, staring at a place on the bar in front of me.

Her perfume was strong, but not overpowering. Nice, attractive, like the woman wearing it.

"You're a P. I., aren't you?"

"How do you know that?"

She placed a tattered, worn business card on the bar. It had a pinhole on the top where it had been pinned to the bulletin board in the vestibule between the outer and inner doors of this bar. It was an old card.

"Surely, you can do better than hiring me," I said, taking a sip of my drink.

"I can't afford better."

I looked at her through whiskey-soaked eyes.

"Are you buttering me up?"

"I'm offering you a job if you're sober enough to listen to the details," she said.

I downed my drink in one sip, motioning for the bartender to bring me another. I did not like this woman anymore.

"I have a case that will pull you out of this sewer you find yourself in."

"This bar ain't so bad," I said, smiling at Amanda as she set my drink down. She shook her head and moved on.

"I'm not talking about the bar. I'm talking about your life."

I stared at her for a moment.

"What do you know about anything?"

"I know you used to be a good cop and a good investigator. I know that now you spend your days here drinking and not doing anything that involves much effort. I know your so-called company is on its last legs and so might you be, too."

I took a sip.

"Guess you know a lot then."

"You want to hear about this case?"

"You buying the drinks?"

"I'm buying the coffee," she said, motioning Amanda over.

I was feeling a bit conflicted. I either wanted to run away as fast as I could from her, or I wanted to marry her.

# 2

We took our coffee cups to a corner table so we could be separated from the few patrons. I sipped the hot coffee, wishing I had a slug of whiskey for flavor. She was busy spreading photos and papers out on the table.

"I don't even know your name," I said.

"Sarah Collier," she said, not looking up from her task.

"I'm Joe Langley."

She stopped sorting her files and looked up.

"Yeah, I know that. Remember?"

She went back to sorting papers; I was fuming inside. I was perfectly content sitting at the bar, getting blind drunk, and feeling sorry for myself. I didn't need this, but she, Sarah, was that her name? She said something about a payday. It had been a while since I had a good one of those.

"OK! Now, what I have here is a timeline. It shows every move the bastard who killed my sister has made since her death," she said, spreading her arms wide to take in the paperwork spread across the table.

"Killed?"

"Yes."

I sat down in the chair opposite her. She was watching me look at the paperwork.

"What's wrong with you?"

"I haven't worked a murder in a long time," I said.

"Well, this is a cold case. You ever worked one of them?"

I looked at her but said nothing. Cold cases were usually a no-win situation. If you found new evidence, it usually was not enough for an arrest, much less a trial. Rare occasions aside.

"I don't understand," I said.

"I know that," she said, her tone of voice indicating I was simple-minded. "That's why we are going over everything. You sure you're okay to do this now?"

I wasn't sure. I also wasn't going to tell her that.

She picked up a photo from the table and handed it to me. It was of a young girl in her teens. All smiles, with her braces shining, she was starting to get enough acne that more makeup would be needed to hide the transition from girl to woman. The picture was not recent.

"My sister. Her name is Diana. She's thirteen in that photo. It was a school photo for the yearbook. Her last one," Sarah said, taking the photo back.

I looked at her. I was curious now.

"What happened?"

"Right before her fourteenth birthday, she disappeared. She was always shooting baskets at the local basketball court. She wanted to make the team so bad. I was sixteen at the time. I always made fun of her for being a tomboy. One night she didn't come home. We all went looking for her, called our friends and neighbors. Nobody knew where she was."

She was staring at the picture like she was hoping it would tell her something new.

"What did the police say?"

"They did what they could. No trace of her was ever found. When I got of age, I called every month to check on the progress, but eventually, detectives transferred out or retired. The new cops didn't have time to look for a missing kid who had been missing for years. I stopped calling and started looking into it myself."

"You gathered all this information?" I said, pointing at the table of paperwork.

"Me and other private investigators, yeah. Eventually, just me. I had to save money to hire them as I went," she said.

While talking about her sister, her voice lost the snarky tone. I had a feeling that tone was just a cover to hide emotions she didn't want to deal with.

"If you already worked with other investigators, why come to me?"

"They won't take the case anymore. They say there is nothing else they can do."

"And you think I can help?"

"I don't know. I will be honest with you, though. The payday isn't that grand, I lied about that. I may have to mortgage my house or sell a kidney just to pay you. I know that some of the other investigators I used told me you were good at one time. Maybe the best. They told me where to find you."

"These others told you I would take the case?"

"Actually, they said if I could find you and dry you out, you might be able to help. They also said your best days were way behind you," she said, looking straight at me.

I smiled.

"That doesn't offend you?"

"No. It's true, mostly anyway." I sipped my coffee.

Sarah looked at me a moment longer, then picked up another photo from the table. This one was a mugshot photo. An old one.

"This is Ralph Norris. He is a sex offender who lived in our neighborhood. That was before strict registration, so no one knew he was a pervert. He was living there at the time Diana disappeared," she said.

"Any reason to think he did it?"

"The timeline makes sense. Look," she said, handing me a spiral notebook. "Turn to page seventy-four. The numbers are on the top."

I turned the pages, scanning as I did so. It was a journal detailing the whereabouts of Ralph Norris at the time of Diana Collier's disappearance. It was put together well with no time missing or unaccounted for. I found page seventy-four.

My buzz from the scotch was wearing off. I wanted to help find this missing girl, dead girl, I told myself. Diana was dead. Nobody stayed missing this long. Which reminded me of a question.

"How old would she be now?"

"Thirty-six."

I let out a low whistle. She had been missing for twenty-two years. That was a lifetime ago. Way too long to hold out hope she was alive. Sarah must have read my mind.

"I know she's probably dead, Joe. I just want to find the man who killed her."

I looked around the smoky bar, trying to convince myself this was not the case to work on. Especially for someone whose reputation was already in the sewer.

I looked over at Sarah. She was looking at me as if I were her last hope.

"You want to get out of here and go for a walk," I said, standing up.

# 3

It was a warm night for spring. There was no breeze blowing from the ocean, the air was still. The humidity caused my shirt to cling to me like I had stepped from the shower after bathing fully clothed.

We walked easily, slowly around the block. We didn't look at each other. I looked around at buildings and streets I had seen a thousand times before as if seeing them for the first time. Sarah stared at a spot on the sidewalk that was always in front of her.

Downtown was deserted at this hour. It gave me the feeling that we had the entire island to ourselves. Sarah looked over at me, then said,

"I want to find her, give her a decent burial, and give my parents closure."

"There is no such thing as closure. It's all a myth, made-up psychobabble."

Sarah kept talking as if she didn't hear me.

"My folks have argued with me over this for a while. They say I'm wasting my life looking for the killer."

"Are you?"

She shrugged her shoulders and sighed.

"I don't know. Someone must do it. I would hate for Diana to just be forgotten about. I'm not married, I have no hobbies to speak of. I just want to know what happened to my sister."

We walked in silence for a bit longer. The thick file folder had been tucked under her arm, she took it and held it out in front of her as if it were a serving tray.

"All my efforts are in this file. If I can't find out for sure what happened to Diana, then I have wasted my life."

We made it around the block back to the front of the bar. I looked at her in the glow of the streetlights which cast shadows on her face, a tear glowed here and there.

"I will take the file. I'll look it over tomorrow and get back with you the day after. How's that sound?"

She handed me the file and nodded, exhaling deeply.

"My phone number and address are in the front of the notebook. I would appreciate any help at all," she said.

We walked her to her car in silence. Her car was an old Honda. The paint was faded, and the car fenders were dented in.

"You need a ride?"

"My place isn't far."

I watched her drive away. I felt energized for a moment. I had something to look into that wasn't a cheating spouse or a child custody issue.

My office was two blocks down, above a business, so I walked there. I spent more time in the office than I did in my apartment.

I felt the weight of the file as I carried it. There would be no sleep tonight. I would be working. I felt good for a change.

# 4

The next morning, I was up by eight with my coffee cup in hand. I sat at my desk and picked up the file, opened it to the first page of the notebook Sarah had shown me last night.

I sipped my coffee, which was a little bitter. From the desk drawer, I pulled a bottle out and splashed a little whiskey in the coffee. It tasted much better. I began reading.

Diana Collier was two months shy of her fourteenth birthday when she disappeared. Her last sighting had been at a basketball court in the area where she lived. Her playing basketball, either alone or with local kids, was a common sight according to neighbors the police had talked to.

On page seventy-three, Ralph Norris' mugshot was staring at me. He was a young man, almost a kid when he was arrested. The man in the photo looked embarrassed as well as mad.

He was, at the time of Diana's disappearance, living six houses down from the Collier's house. I turned the page.

Norris' arrest record was stapled to the notebook pages. It appeared to be a computer printout from a website. I poured

13

more coffee and whiskey and kept reading. Norris only had one arrest to go with the mugshot. In 1988, he had been arrested for sexual assault of a child.

The victim was sixteen and Norris was…I checked his date of birth, nineteen.

The next page was a copy of the police report. Names redacted. I read carefully. Norris and the sixteen-year-old, whose name was not in the file, met at a restaurant she had been working at. According to Norris, she told him she was seventeen, the age of consent in the State. They spoke often when he was in the restaurant, then things went too far.

There was no statement from Norris, other than the police report, about the events of the incident.

I put the file down. This girl was sixteen when she met Norris. She was still alive. And Norris had never been in trouble for anything again. He was not on the sex offender registry because he had served his time. His sentence had been probation for five years and a fine and community service.

I fired up my computer. Checking names on the internet and doing a property search of county records, I found an address for Ralph Norris. He no longer lived at the address in the folder. I printed the current address out.

I glanced at my watch. It was noon. I had finished the pot of coffee and was feeling the effects of the whiskey, the splashes had gotten more liberal as I drank the coffee. I grabbed my keys and headed out the door.

# 5

Ralph Norris lived in a nice neighborhood in the suburbs. The house must have cost two hundred grand if a penny. I stared at the rock walkway leading to the front door. The manicured grass and the landscaping were meticulous.

There was a nice BMW sitting in the driveway. It was as perfect as the yard. I felt out of place in my old Ford pickup, like a trespasser that would soon be found and run off.

I knocked on the front door and waited. I could hear movement from inside the house. No dogs barking, not that I would have expected any in this house.

The man who answered the front door looked at me like he knew I was that trespasser he was warned about. I shook the feeling off.

"Ralph Norris?"

He nodded.

He was approaching fifty, with grey hair thinning toward baldness. He was overweight, carrying it mostly in the gut.

"Joe Langley," I said. giving him my card, the same one Sarah had placed in front of me last night.

He looked at it, then looked at me. His attitude shifted. I could feel it.

"What do you want? I am sick of talking to you people," he said.

"If it happens often, then you know why I am here. You got a few minutes?"

I was hoping he would let me in, but he just stood there looking at me.

"I am looking into the Collier case now. What can you tell me about that?"

He sighed, "I can tell you that if you are here talking to me, then you are as lost as the others who have harassed me over the years. I am tired of it."

"Maybe I'm not as lost as you think."

That caught him off guard.

"Oh! Why is that?"

"Because you're innocent," I said.

He looked at me for a long moment. He stepped aside and invited me in. I followed into a living room that was as nicely furnished as one would expect. No second-hand furniture or rent to own either.

After we sat down, I looked at him and noticed the beginning of tears forming in the corner of his eyes.

"I looked over the file like I said. I don't think you had anything to do with this girl's disappearance."

"I didn't. I have been telling that to people off and on for years and years," he said.

"Do you remember seeing that girl in the neighborhood back then?"

"Sure. She was always running around. Usually with a basketball. I knew her folks a little. It was a close neighborhood until she went missing."

"When did you become a focus of the investigation?"

"Right after. The police found my arrest and hounded me. Then the other daughter, Sarah, took up the cause. For over twenty years, I have had a parade of people questioning me, like I'm hiding something. You are the first one to say you think I'm innocent."

"You only have the one arrest because of the girl who worked at the restaurant?"

He stood, smiling. He walked to the fireplace, took a picture from the mantle, and handed it to me.

"This is the girl from the restaurant," he said.

It was a wedding photo. I stared at it, then looked at him.

"She's at work right now. Liberty Hospital. She's a doctor."

# 6

I needed a drink. I told myself I'd have only one, then I would go talk to Sarah. The Clover Leaf was nearly empty when I walked in since it was only a little past two in the afternoon.

Amanda, saw me come in and had my drink waiting at the bar when I got to my usual seat. I downed it quick, then two more. I nursed the next one.

A few hours later, I realized I was nearly drunk. I had Amanda call me a cab, then waited outside for it to arrive. It was nearly eight o'clock.

I stayed too long and drank too much. If life had a slogan for each person, that would be mine.

I leaned on the doorjamb and knocked on the apartment door. Sarah opened it, staring at me.

No bra. That was the first thing I noticed as she opened the door. Sarah was wearing a loose-fitting tank top that struggled to contain her breasts. I felt myself smiling at her stupidly.

"Thought we agreed to meet tomorrow," she said, allowing me to follow her into the apartment.

Her shorts were so short you could see the curvature of her hips. I gladly followed her into the apartment.

"I have some news," I said, looking around.

The apartment was small, the living room and kitchen were combined, separated by a small bar. The small couch had stuffing coming out of the cushions. A coffee table had an array of different liquor bottles on it, all at various levels of empty.

She went to the kitchen and retrieved a glass. She poured Jack Daniels in her glass, then filled another that she handed to me.

I drank it down fast. She refilled it, looking at me strangely.

"What news?"

I sat on the couch, sipping my drink, silent for a moment. The room was spinning, and my eyes had trouble focusing on what I was looking at.

"I spoke to Ralph Norris today."

"So soon," she said.

"He is not a viable suspect. Never has been," I said. I heard my words slur.

"He is a pervert. He got in trouble for…"

I interrupted.

"No. Not a pervert. The girl he got in trouble for, he married. He's still married to her. She's a doctor."

"That can't be."

"It is. He has told all this to investigators in the past. They all knew it. Someone has been lying to you if they kept chasing this man."

She sat silent for a moment, then started talking again. I listened for a minute, but somewhere in her talking, I passed out.

# 7

I awoke slowly, a catch in my neck. My head was slumped over, I was still sitting up. My head felt like a weight was holding it down, my mouth was full of cotton.

I saw a half-full Jim Beam bottle on the coffee table. I took a long pull from it. I felt a little better, so I took another drink.

Slowly, I stood and walked past the kitchen down a small hallway. A bathroom was on the right, the bedroom straight ahead. I looked in the bedroom.

Sarah was asleep on top of the blankets in the clothes she wore last night. I went to the bathroom.

When I opened the door, Sarah was standing in the hallway, looking at me. Her hair was a mess, and she looked half asleep. Her right eye was closed, the left eye was looking at me

"Want some coffee?" she asked.

The aftereffects of a drunken night hung heavy in the air, foul-smelling, and dark.

I followed her back to the kitchen. I leaned on the bar while she made coffee.

"I usually don't sleep with men on the first meeting as a rule," she said, smiling.

"Technically, this is the second meeting, so no rules were broken. And I don't think passing out counts as sleeping, anyway."

She giggled. We were silent as she made the coffee. She handed me a cup and filled one for herself.

"How many investigators have you had looking at this case?" I asked, sipping the hot liquid.

"Five maybe. Over the years," she said.

"Norris told me he has talked to a lot of people over the years. He told them the same thing he told me. If so, then I think these people have lied to you," I said.

She looked at me over her coffee cup rim. "No way. They all say he was a good suspect, but…"

"But they needed more money to chase more leads. Right?"

"Yeah!"

"Scam. Sorry, Sarah, you have been scammed. How much did you lose?"

"I refinanced my house, then sold it. I have been trying to save to hire another one when I was given your name."

"Why me?"

"The police detective told me you were a fair guy for a lush." She looked at me to see if the insult had any effect. "If anything was there, you'd tell me. And you wouldn't be too expensive, given your situation."

"This detective, who is he?"

"Detective Webster."

"I know James. I'll go talk to him today."

She smiled and refilled my cup. The coffee was not helping my sick feeling. I needed food.

"Wanna grab some breakfast?"

She nodded her head.

"I need a ride home afterward," I said.

# 8

The Clover Leaf sat exactly midway between my office and my apartment. I made it to my apartment without feeling the need to stop at the bar. It was closed now anyway.

Sarah dropped me off outside and we agreed to meet later. Once inside, I poured a scotch from the bottle on the counter to help clear the fogginess of the previous night. I then showered and changed clothes, sipping my drink slowly.

I sat on my couch, looking around the room, considering my next move. My apartment was sparse. A single couch, a small side table next to it, and an old TV that I didn't even know worked or not.

I shook my head in frustration. I knew what I needed to do and was putting it off. I picked up the house phone, listened for a dial tone, hoping I had paid the bill this month.

I called the police department to set up a meeting with Detective Webster. I knew James Webster from my time in the police force. He was a ball-breaking sergeant then. He didn't seem happy to be talking to me. He rarely was the few times I'd see him. There was too much history. I told him what I was working on. He agreed to meet at Rioli's for lunch.

He was seated at a table, waiting for me when I arrived. He was an imposing figure, all six feet of him, as he sat there in his suit and tie. He looked the part of a detective straight from central casting.

His hair was thinner, his gut was thicker, but he was still a cop through and through.

"Sorry, I'm late," I said, sitting down.

We did not shake hands.

"I ordered for you," he said.

There was a water glass in front of me. I took a drink.

"What do you think of Sarah Collier?" he asked.

"I'm just getting started looking into the missing sister. I spoke to Ralph Norris. I don't think he is a good suspect."

"No kidding." He stared at me like I was his errant child. "We eliminated him as a suspect years ago. She keeps hanging onto it because the washed-up investigators she hires tell her to."

He took a long drink of his tea.

"Any other suspects worth talking to?" I asked.

"You're the hotshot P.I. You tell me?"

"Could I look at the case file?"

"She has a copy. Should anyway. One of the investigators did an open record on it," he said.

"Probably redacted. I want to see it, the whole file," I said.

Our food arrived. He had ordered a nice lasagna for himself; it made my stomach growl from hunger. The waiter set a plate of octopus in front of me. I gave Webster what I hoped was a withering look. He ignored me.

"Let's eat. Then we will see what we can see," he said.

I wasn't hungry.

# 9

I followed Webster into the police station. I hated coming here for various reasons. I had spent a lot of my years in this building working for the city but left under a cloud of doubt as to my character.

I still knew some of the officers working here, but like anything else, it always felt different coming back. It reminded me of an old saying that if you leave policing, it's like you were never in it and if you ever come back to it, it's like you were never gone.

But I was gone. I had been for a long time. While in my investigator's work, I maintained a relationship with the police department, it was at arm's length. Now, I felt like I was walking into a den of lions. I hoped they weren't hungry.

We made our way past the reception area into the main part of the building where the offices were. I kept my head down and followed Webster. Inside his office, he motioned for me to sit in the chair in front of his desk.

"The file is here somewhere. I was looking at it as I spoke with Sarah Collier," he said.

He fumbled through a stack of folders on his desk. He handed me a blue folder that felt light to me.

"This is it?" I said.

The folder was thin for a case that had been opened for over two decades.

"All I got," he said.

"I've seen trespassing cases with more paperwork. Are you sure?"

"Don't be a wiseass. You want to see the file or not," he said, reaching to take the file back.

I opened it and started looking through it. There was not as much as one would think with a twenty-year old cold case. There was the initial dispatch sheet that sent officers to the address. The papers were old, the forms that were used before my time with the department.

The sheet showed detectives had been called an hour after arriving on the scene. The notes for the detective's actions were minimal.

More notes on index cards showed little activity after the first month of investigation. The file did not contain any information about Ralph Norris. I mentioned that to Webster.

"It's in there. Gotta be," he said, leaning back in his chair.

I looked again. It was not.

"Sarah has a copy of this?"

"How do I know what Sarah has?"

"Can I get a copy of this?"

"Sure. For a quarter a page and allow ten days for it to be completed," he said.

I thought I detected an extra level of hostility in Webster's voice, but with him, it was hard to tell.

"You mad at me for something?"

"No. Not at all, just that you spend most of your days blind drunk and now you want to second guess the work of cops you could never be like," he said, standing. "What's to be angry about?"

"You recommended me to her," I said.

"Yeah. I was hoping she would see what kind of bum you were and not hire you. She has worn out every decent private investigator in this city."

I stood and dropped the file on his desk.

"How decent could they be, if the prime suspect they have been chasing for two decades is not valid? And the police file mentions nothing about talking to Norris," I said.

Webster stood to face me. We were about the same height; I was maybe a bit taller.

"You know what your problem is, Langley? You blew onto the island like storm debris from a hurricane. You aren't from here, though you act like you are. You've never fit in with the locals, the movers and shakers of this island. You're just a useless drunk. Now, get the hell outta my office."

I stared at Webster for a long moment, then turned and walked out. I hated coming to this place.

# 10

I went for a drive to clear my head. My meeting with Webster had gone about like all the other times we had to meet. He didn't like me, and I didn't like him.

I ended up where I always went when I needed to think. The Clover Leaf. The nice thing about day drinking is you miss the evening crowds, and there was none when I got to the bar.

Amanda waited until I sat down to make me a scotch on the rocks, she set the drink in front of me.

Amanda had been a bartender at this place for four or five years. In her mid-twenties, brown hair, some tattoos that seemed to be a younger generational thing, she was a pretty girl, a woman. She had a daughter that she had to support on her bar pay.

At times, I felt guilty for not paying my tab like I should have. I usually drank until the feeling passed though.

Now, I needed to let a different feeling pass.

The case file bothered me. Or to be more precise, the lack of a case file bothered me.

There should be more to the file than what Webster had shown me. The case was over twenty years old, yet it looked as if not much work had gone into it after the initial investigation.

I had more questions than answers. And it seemed no one wanted to provide any answers. Maybe there were no answers.

Children disappear all over the country for various reasons. Sometimes the authorities never know the reasons. I thought of the thin folder I had held in my hands. The case file Webster called it.

Amanda set another drink in front of me and took my empty glass. She dumped the ice and washed the glass.

"You got a job lined up, I heard."

"Did it make the papers? How did you hear that?"

"Bartenders gossip, you know."

"I always wondered who a bartender told their secrets and problems to"

"Sarah Collier, huh?"

I looked at Amanda, my glass halfway to my mouth froze in midair.

"How do you know that?"

"I heard it was a missing person's case from a long time ago. The other bartender, Mike, told me. He described the woman."

"Describing doesn't equal a name."

"I knew Sarah when I was younger. When I worked at a different bar. Never laid eyes on her before. The lady is famous in a lot of bars. She was obsessed with her sister's case even then, so I heard."

She moved off to tend to other duties. I sipped my drink and thought about Sarah. She had been chasing a dead end for years and other investigators had been allowing it, lying to her about what they needed and were doing.

I made a scotch-soaked vow to never lie to the woman. That was a promise I meant to keep.

# 11

When I left the Clover Leaf, I had no destination in mind. I had business to attend to, but I wasn't exactly clear eyed and level-headed.

I drove to the address that was listed in the file Sarah had given me. The address of Sarah's parents. I had no idea if they still lived in that house, but I wanted to see the neighborhood and get a feel for the location.

Every crime, whether that crime is a murder or as simple as a stolen wallet, has a scene, and that scene needs to be investigated and studied. After twenty or so years, I hoped there was something left of this scene to study.

The house was in an area of the city known as Big Beach, where the upper middle class lived and raised their children in safety from the crime and filth of downtown. The average cost of a house in this neighborhood was more money than I had made in my life. I already felt out of place.

I pulled my old pickup over to the curb and sat across the street from the address. My truck stood out like a sore thumb in this neighborhood.

I made my way up the walkway to the front door of the house. The house was wood framed, built on stilts. I wondered how many hurricanes it had seen in its life. The bottom was a garage and workshop, the two upper floors serving as the living area.

The front yard was well manicured, and the house was well maintained. I rang the doorbell and listened to it chime. Before the chime faded the door was answered by a woman in her mid-sixties who was as well manicured as the lawn. She greeted me with a smile.

"Mrs. Collier?"

"Yes?"

"I'm Joe Langley. I'm working for Sarah looking into the case of your daughter. Is now a good time?"

She invited me in, reluctantly.

"You are the new investigator?" she said, leading me through the house to the living room.

"Yes. Did Sarah mention me?"

"Oh, no. We haven't spoken to Sarah in quite some time. We have disagreements as to her endeavors," she said, motioning me to a straight back chair.

I sat down.

"What do you mean?"

"I'll let my husband, Ben, tell you," she said continuing down a small hall.

When she returned, a man followed behind her. He was fit and dressed well. We shook hands and he motioned me to sit back down. The wife disappeared to the kitchen.

He was in his sixties and appeared to never miss a hair appointment or a tanning session. His white hair was thick and full, cut above the ears, his skin a tanned brown. He wore no tie, but looked dressed for a meeting, nonetheless.

"Marie tells me you are now looking into the Diana case," he said.

He said it as if it was something he was following in the papers.

"Yes sir. I am hoping to find something Sarah hasn't been able to find out."

"Like what?"

"Well, I already know Ralph Norris, your former neighbor, is not a good suspect."

Ben laughed. I was confused.

"Forgive me, Mr. Langley. Mr. Norris has not been a viable suspect for years. The police eliminated him almost immediately."

"Sarah said some of the other private investigators have been looking at him and checking him out. Norris confirmed that when we spoke," I said.

"I'm sure. The people Sarah hired were not exactly poster boys for ethical behavior. No insult intended. She has squandered what money she had hiring those folks."

"Is that the source of your disagreements?"

He looked at me full on.

"Your wife told me you hadn't spoken to Sarah in a while," I said.

"Yes, well, I guess so. I saw you pull up in that old pickup out front. Judging by your vehicle, the liquor on your breath, and your appearance of someone who hasn't seen prosperous times in a while, you may be no better than the others she has foolishly hired," he said.

I took no offense to his statement. I was wondering if maybe he was right.

Ben Collier stood, I did too. He led me to the front door and opened it.

"Have a good day, Mr. Langley. And don't come back here again," he said.

I walked back to my vehicle confused by his reactions and mad at not pushing for answers.

# 12

After leaving the Collier house, I drove around and looked for the basketball court where Diane was playing the night she disappeared. I could not find it. It was not within a six-block radius of the Collier house. I drove around in circles, trying to locate the court. I gave up after thirty minutes of searching.

I drove back to the Clover Leaf. It was just past six o'clock, and I needed a drink and some time alone to think about the day. Amanda was working and had my drink waiting for me when I sat down at the empty bar.

I drank it down as she came back with another. The visit to the Collier house was a strange one. It would seem they would want to find out what happened to their daughter. But maybe after two decades, they had closed the book on that as something they would never know. It had to be hard to keep picking at the scab of the wound every time a new investigator took over the case.

Why had Sarah spent all her money and sold her house to keep the case alive? After so many years, a person loses hope, no matter who that person is. Hope is fleeting.

The investigators she had hired had misled her, or so it seemed. Webster had said Sarah had hired every P.I. on the island at one time or another. I needed to talk to the other P.I. agencies she had hired. I sipped my drink.

I lost track of my drinks and the time because I realized Sarah was sitting beside me. She had quietly come in and sat down just like she had on our first meeting. I made a mental note to be more attentive.

"You visited my parents?" she asked.

She didn't seem angry. She seemed resigned.

"Guess y'all are talking now," I said, sipping my drink.

She ordered one of her own as Amanda fixed me another.

"You should have told me you were going to do that."

"I need to see the neighborhood, talk to people who were there at the time," I said.

She nodded, "I know, but my parents are weird about this. They think I have wasted my time."

"Maybe you have. And your money, too. Your dad knew about Norris not being a suspect. So did the police. Why are you chasing it so hard when everyone I've talked to eliminated him years ago?"

"I was told it made sense," she said.

"You were lied to. And you are lying to yourself. You should throw the whole Norris file in the trash. That's where it belongs."

"I just want to know what happened to my sister. If I go broke and homeless, I'm okay with that," she said.

I didn't want to argue, not now when I had a good buzz going. I changed the subject.

"I need to know all the other agencies you hired."

"I'll give you a list. It's everyone on the island, though. I'll text it," she said as she stood. "Don't bother my parents anymore."

"Call the office, leave a message. I don't have a cellphone."

She walked away. I could tell she was upset. I didn't know why. I did know her drink arrived. I kept my buzz going.

# 13

The first thing I noticed when I awoke was, I was in my apartment. The next thought was the conversation I'd had with Sarah Collier. Was it an argument? Why was she so defensive about me speaking with her parents?

The parents seemed convinced that Sarah was wasting her time and money keeping the investigation open, looking for her sister. The parents had known Ralph Norris was not a suspect, so why were Sarah and the other investigators trying to make him one?

The investigators Sarah had hired were another topic all together. There were only so many of us on the island. Most were good, hard-working investigators. Some were like me, just hanging on, and others were sleazy, in the worst form of that word. That would be my next step.

I needed to speak with the last investigator Sarah hired. That would clear up a lot of this confusion. Maybe.

I showered, brushed my teeth, and dressed while thinking of all this. I looked around my small efficiency apartment that I called home.

There were liquor bottles on the cabinet by the refrigerator. Some full, most empty. In my small living area were more bottles in similar condition. I decided to quit, well to cut back, on drinking until this case was over. I knew I wouldn't, and it didn't bother me.

I found my cordless phone. Checked for a dial tone. I called Sarah's cell phone number. No answer. I needed to talk to her this morning. I left a voice message telling her I would be at the office later.

I needed food now. Then I would get to work on the case and find some answers.

# 14

After I had breakfast, I drove to the Collier neighborhood again. Not to visit the parents, I stayed away from their house. But to see if I could find the basketball court Diana was supposedly playing on when she disappeared. I had not found it earlier.

This time, I asked Captain Webster to meet me to show me the neighborhood. We had not parted on good terms, but we seldom did, even when I was a police officer. But I had known him for a long time, and despite how we felt about each other, I trusted his judgment. I wanted to get his thoughts on the matter.

Webster pulled in behind me. I got out and met him between our cars. He still seemed agitated.

"Hope this isn't a waste of my time, Langley."

He didn't offer to shake hands, so I didn't push it.

"You know where the playground was back then?"

"I got a drawing from the file," he said.

"I didn't see a drawing in the file," I said.

"No? I bet you miss a lot nowadays."

I considered that for a moment. I had not seen a drawing in the file I had looked at in his office. Webster pretending that I missed it irked me a bit.

He pointed toward the south.

"The playground was over there."

"It's not now," I said.

We started walking in silence. Webster was looking down at the drawing, then back up. After three blocks, he stopped.

"What difference does this make now?"

"What?" I asked, confused by the question.

"The girl went missing from a basketball court that has been replaced by a fountain, see?"

He pointed to a water fountain in a little park. The park had a walking trail and a picnic area with benches in various places. It took up maybe three-quarters of an acre of land.

"How far are we from the girl's house?"

"Three blocks. We know she was last seen here. We don't know how, or from where she went missing," he said.

"The original detective? Maybe I can talk to him."

"Sure. You'll need a Ouija board and a medium to do that. He died a few years back."

"What was his name?"

"Did you hear me? He died," Webster said.

I looked at him.

"Reeves. Bob Reeves."

I took one last look around the park and the neighborhood. I left Webster standing there as I walked back to my car alone. Where did he get the drawing he was looking at? It wasn't in the file. There seemed to be no decent answers to any of the questions that circulated around this case.

# 15

I wanted to talk to Sarah again, but I remembered how we left it the last time we had spoken at the Clover Leaf. I was hoping she wasn't still mad. It was only a quarter to five, so I drove to her apartment.

I knocked on her door thirty minutes later. I heard something fall inside. I moved my head toward the door, listening.

Sarah opened the door, and the smell of booze hit me full force. Her eyes were glassy and red, like she had been crying. She invited me in, then offered me a drink, which I accepted.

She poured me a glass of whiskey as I told her my story of visiting the neighborhood where Diana was last seen.

She listened without comment, handing me the glass of liquor, and sat beside me on the couch.

"So, we are nowhere?"

"Yeah. For now," I said.

"I have been thinking," she said, looking down at her glass. "I think my parents are right. I have wasted my money and time trying to find out about my sister's disappearance."

"If you want to stop, that's up to you. I think it would bear looking into a little more. And you aren't paying me yet so you're not out anything," I said.

She looked up at me. I grabbed the bottle of whiskey from the coffee table and poured another drink for myself. I drank it in one swallow.

"OK. If you think so," she said.

"It's a fountain now," I said, getting me a refill of whiskey.

She looked at me strangely.

"The basketball court? It's a fountain in a little park, now," I said.

"Yeah. I know. My father was the one in the neighborhood that led the way to get rid of the courts and put something better there."

The whiskey was affecting me. I was feeling the start of a buzz. I liked that feeling.

Sarah was half passed out. She kept leaning her head back against the couch cushion. She was having trouble talking and slurring her words.

I watched her for a moment. Her eyes closed. I waited, sipping more whiskey. She slumped over on the couch, her head on the arm, her feet on the floor.

I waited a few minutes, then I went exploring. I wanted to see what I could learn about this woman, her family, and anything else I could find.

Since there were no pictures on the walls or on the TV stand, I started there. I quietly searched the living area for photo albums or pictures of any kind. There were none.

Making my way to the bedroom, I checked the closet for anything that looked like a keepsake box or storage container. Still nothing.

After about forty-five minutes of looking around and finding nothing, I was feeling frustrated. She lived in this apartment without a single memento of her past.

I had two more drinks while I searched. Sarah maintained her position on the couch, neither moving nor making a sound.

Finally, I left the apartment, leaving Sarah where she was. I knew no more now than I did when the day started. I wanted a drink.

# 16

More than a drink, I wanted to talk to the last investigator Sarah had hired to work on this case. Some were good, but some were not the most ethical.

For my purposes, I needed to talk to just one of them. And when it came to unethical, no one was more so than Peter Connolly.

Pete Connolly had been a cop, way before my time, who was busted out for Brady violations. He had withheld pertinent evidence from the prosecution in a case, knowing the defense would not have the opportunity to see it.

Brady vs. Maryland was the reigning court case on that behavior, which when summarized says, lie to the lawyers, you become a sleaze ball private investigator whom nobody trusts.

Not nobody. Apparently, Sarah trusted him. Maybe Peter Connolly had turned over a new leaf. I would soon find out.

The whiskey I drank at Sarah's was wearing off, which was a good thing. I needed fresh faculties to speak with

Connolly, who could be aggravating in even the best of circumstances.

I pulled in front of his office building, a split-level complex where rent was more than most P.I.'s make in a month. I didn't know how he got his money or where he got his clients, but I did know there were rumors he did a lot of work for different criminal organizations, both in this state and others.

Peter Connolly was a sixty something year old man who tried hard to erase the hands of time. He acted like a man twenty years younger, the way he talked and dressed.

His secretary announced my presence, I heard him say show me in. I was annoyed already. He had a real-life secretary, a nice office, and a client list that never ran dry. He was housed in an office I could never afford. It was enough to make me wonder which of us was the sleazeball investigator?

He stood from behind his big ornate desk, extending his hand while smiling.

"Joe, it has been a long time. How are you?"

"Making it," I said, taking the offered hand. I was the picture of polite. We sat.

His office was decorated in bright colors, with pictures of oil wells and horses on the wall.

"How can I help you?"

I told him about Sarah Collier and her case. He nodded and made the right noises in the right spots. I wanted to punch him.

"Anyway, I thought maybe she had hired you at one point and you could tell me something useful."

"I did some work for her," he said, as he pushed his intercom.

The secretary, all pert and put together well, came in from the other room. He asked for the file. She went to a file cabinet in the corner of the office and pulled out a folder, handing it to him, then left.

"Strange girl, Sarah. You know?" he said, flipping the file open.

"Strange how?"

He handed me a stack of papers.

"She's an alcoholic. Bad drunk. And, sadly, when she binges, she sees ghosts. And expects you to chase them."

I came to a piece of paper with a woman's handwriting. A list of several names. I held it up for Connolly to see.

"Ghosts," he said. "People she thinks are suspects she wanted me to check out."

"Did you?"

"At first. Before I knew better. Those names on that list are just random people. Strangers mainly. They never even heard of the Colliers or what happened to Diana. Some weren't even born when the girl went missing."

My face gave me away; I could feel my eyebrows raise. I stared down at the list.

"You have talked to her, right? Does she seem normal to you?" he asked.

I didn't trust myself to answer. I asked my own question.

"Ralph Norris. She thinks he is a suspect. I don't. You talk to him?"

"First person I interviewed. At her insistence. Did she show you the pervert file of him? It was a dead end, like the names on that list. Pure smoke," he said.

I stood to leave. I handed him back the paperwork.

"When did she hire you?"

"Six months ago, maybe."

"She told me she hadn't hired anyone in a while, she had no money."

I had my hand on the doorknob, his voice stopped me.

"I'm sure she doesn't, the way she lives. Her mother paid my fee."

I was more confused than before as I was leaving Connolly's office.

# 17

I didn't know what to make of my talk with Connolly. When I spoke with Sarah's parents, they appeared frustrated their daughter was spending so much time and money on the search for what happened to Diana. So, why had her mother paid the fee to Connolly?

I felt at odds. Sarah obviously had her problems. Then again, so did I. I surely would not hold drinking against anyone.

I pulled my pickup to the curb in front of my office. Compared to Connolly's office, it was not much to look at. My office was above a bakery, the smell of freshly baked bread was strong.

He was waiting for me in front of the door to the stairs that led to my office. Slouchy clothes, his hair that was still there going gray, his shoes worn down. If you didn't know better, a person would think he was down on his luck.

Mickey Holt owned the building. The bakery was always on time with rent. Me, not so much.

I tried to recall if I had paid this month's rent and couldn't remember if I had paid last month's either.

He was a real estate investor who had inherited most of his property from his late father. Despite his style of dress, Mickey Holt was worth a lot of money.

"Mick, what brings you down here?" I asked as I walked up to unlock the outer door.

"Checking on my building. Thought I'd visit a little," he said.

"Do I owe rent?"

"I don't think so. I heard you had a new client," he said.

"How'd you hear that?"

"Girl's father is a friend of mine," he said, following me upstairs.

"I'm doing this pro bono for now."

"You're all heart, that's what I always say."

Mickey Holt rarely dropped by unannounced. When he did, I always felt like it was an invasion of my privacy, like I was being inspected to make sure I was taking care of his building.

Once inside, I looked for anything I should try to hide. Like empty bottles or dirty underwear. Seeing it was a lost cause to hide anything, I offered him a seat.

He looked around and shook his head, not wanting to sit.

"How well do you know the Colliers?" I asked.

"Ben Collier has been a friend of mine for years. We have done business off and on over time. I don't know the wife, Marie, very well," he said.

"Sarah thinks she has a lead on her sister. She wanted me to find out if it was good or not. I'm just getting started," I said.

"So, you aren't being paid for your time?"

I shook my head.

"No, we haven't discussed price."

Mickey scratched his neck and shrugged, "Sarah has...problems. You are aware, right?"

"I think she and I suffer the same malady."

He looked at me, then looked around the room.

"We both like our drink," I said, figuring I could read his thoughts.

"Oh! Yes, indeed. But I was talking about her single-minded focus on this issue," he said.

"She wants to know what happened to her sister. I can understand that."

"She has been a source of consternation to her father. My advice is, be careful of her. Look around, when you don't find anything, move on."

"I will take that on advisement."

He walked to the door. Standing in the doorway, he looked back at me.

"Be careful of her flights of fancy, Joe."

He walked out, leaving me more confused as to why he had stopped by. If I didn't know better, I'd think he was trying to warn me off the case.

I made up my mind. I was not going anywhere.

# 18

The next morning, I was still agitated. Mickey Holt didn't just drop in without a reason. Even my being late with rent didn't warrant a visit from him. So, what was his intent on coming by? Was he really just checking in on the building?

I didn't think so. The more I thought about it, the more I knew he was warning me about looking into this case. As a friend to Sarah's father, was he trying to protect the girl?

How did he know Sarah's father? They appeared to be total opposites. I couldn't see Mickey Holt in business with Ben Collier.

I had no answers. And that bothered me a lot. I went back to my office to make phone calls. No one was waiting for me this morning as I parked my truck.

At one time I had a secretary who was very good at not only her job but keeping me in line, as much as she could, anyway. But when jobs got scarce, I had to let her go. Kim Joyce still freelanced for me from time to time, though. I called her from my desk. She would be here in an hour.

I wanted a drink, but since it was only eight-thirty, I settled for going down the street for breakfast. I called Sarah to invite her, No answer.

Over eggs and bacon, I thought about Sarah and her situation. She had lied to me about paying for Peter Connolly. Though a small lie, it begged the question, what else was she lying about? How bad was her drinking problem? How bad was mine?

Back in the office, I found Kim cleaning up. I greeted her happily. She frowned at me. She frowned at me a lot in the old days. She was a pretty woman who tolerated me and did her job well.

"How do you live like this?"

"You get used to it," I said.

She picked up a trash bag, tied it, and placed it by the door. The glass bottles clanged together as she moved the bag. She had organized and filed some papers in the proper places. Though it was tidy and neat, I was afraid I would never find anything again. I filled her in on the case while she worked.

She sat down at what was once her desk. She had cleaned off a space for her stuff.

"So, you got a paying client?"

"Not really. I never asked for money."

Kim shook her head, frowning.

"What do you want me to do?" she asked.

I pointed to a file on the desk. My attempt at making notes.

"Dig. Deep. I want everything you can find on Sarah, her family, and the missing sister."

"Leg work?"

"You do have some of the best in the business," I said, earning a scolding look.

Kim was not yet forty, a few years younger than me, and had a way of using the internet that I would never understand. Research was her specialty.

I headed for the door, telling her I would be back in a few hours.

I figured Ben Collier would be at work, so taking a chance, I drove to the Collier house in Big Beach. I needed answers.

Marie Collier opened the door, a look of surprise on her face.

"What do you want?" she said.

"A few quick questions," I said.

I smiled to disarm her, maybe. She didn't close the door in my face, so I took that as a good sign. She didn't invite me in either.

"I thought from my last visit, that you and your husband were at odds with Sarah hiring private investigators."

She nodded.

"I found out yesterday you paid the fees for Peter Connolly. Does your husband know that?"

Her face changed expression. Confused how I knew this information. She stepped out onto the porch.

"I wanted Sarah to see it was a waste of time. Mr. Connolly agreed, after two months. He cost me a fortune," she said.

"That doesn't make sense, ma'am," I said.

"Well, nothing about Diana's disappearance makes sense. I have no idea what Sarah is hoping to accomplish. Her sister is missing. We had her declared dead years ago."

"Anything you can tell me about the night Diana went missing?"

"Over twenty years ago? No, I told all to the police then. She was late coming from the courts. Ben went to look for her, then we all joined in."

I thanked Mrs. Collier and left with no more answers than what I started with.

I stopped at a pay phone and called the office. I told Kim I needed an address for the widow of Bob Reeves. She put me on hold, then a few minutes later gave me what I wanted.

I headed to the address. I passed a couple of bars on the way. It reminded me I needed a drink.

# 19

The Reeves' house was a pier-and-beam style affair that had been added onto over the years. The lawn was manicured and there was one vehicle, an older Cadillac, in the driveway.

Mrs. Reeves was younger than I expected. Early sixties, slim, her blonde hair showing streaks of silver. I introduced myself and she invited me in.

I sat down and declined anything to drink. I told her why I was there.

"How can I help with that?"

"I was a cop for a while, myself. Did your husband have any old files around here?

Ones he would look at every once in a while?"

"Bob has been gone about five years now, but I think I kept a box of his stuff in the spare room back here," she said, standing.

She led me to a bedroom that was stacked with boxes of paperwork and files. The markings on the boxes showed they were old tax forms and other personal paperwork.

I saw it as she pointed to it. In the far corner, a white banker's box with the words 'COLLIER' written in black marker across the side. I stepped across some of the other boxes to retrieve the box, I removed the top. Diana Collier's photo was on top.

It was not the photo from school like I had seen earlier. Instead, this was a casual photo of Diana playing in the yard with her friends. The innocence of youth was captured forever in her smile.

Mrs. Reeves led me to the table in the kitchen to look at the contents of the box. She left me alone to look at the items. I removed the files.

The first thing I noticed looking at the contents was that the file Bob Reeves had was thicker than the police file I had looked at earlier in Webster's office.

Inside, was paperwork, and interview notes in Bob's handwriting. I tried to read it.

I found the notes that detailed Ralph Norris's interviews. His story in the notes matched what he had told me. Reeves had dismissed him from the start, it seemed.

After an hour of looking through the file, I was nowhere nearer than I had been before interrupting Mrs. Reeves.

I put the paperwork back in the box and closed the lid. Mrs. Reeves was standing in the passageway to the living room. She looked at me as I lifted the box.

"You find what you needed?"

"No, ma'am. I was hoping he had something I could go on," I said.

I carried the box back to the room and placed it in the spot it had been in.

"I'm sorry. Bob didn't bring his work home with him. This is the only case he ever worked on here at the house."

"How did he die, if you don't mind me asking?"

She was silent for a long moment, tears welled in her eyes but didn't fall.

"Car accident. On his way home from talking with that young girl's parents."

"He was still on the job?"

"Yes, he was."

I thanked her and left. She told me to come back if I needed to. I was hoping I wouldn't need to.

# 20

Kim was sitting at her desk when I walked in. The office had been cleaned and a citrus smell filled the air. I looked around as I stopped in front of her desk.

"Well, what did you find out?" I said, ignoring the cleaning job she had done.

She rolled her eyes at me and picked up a spiral notebook that had her written notes in it.

"Sarah Collier quit school in the eleventh grade. Her mother is a homemaker, father was in commercial finance and real estate. Retired officially years ago, has a nice pension. Makes over six figures a year from his investments. Lived in the same house for thirty-nine years," she said, reading her notes.

"Diana?"

"Disappeared when she was shy of fourteen. According to my source at the police department, they looked into it for a couple of years. All leads dried up, and the case fell on the back burner. They put it in the someday file," she said, putting the notebook down.

"Someday we will get a break. I am familiar with that file. Guess that jibes with what Webster told me," I said.

The phone rang before she could respond. She answered, wrote out a message, then hung up.

She handed me the paper.

"Fella wants to meet you at Rioli's tonight at seven," she said.

"Who?"

"Did you hear me get a name?" she said.

I rolled my eyes this time and went to my desk. Which was just across the room from Kim.

I sat at a table in the corner of Rioli's waiting for my mystery guest to arrive. Then, coming into the front entrance, I saw him. Peter Connolly came walking up to the table, a smile on his face.

"Glad you could make it," he said, sitting down.

"I was expecting someone else."

"Well, you get me. I need to talk to you about something," he said, motioning to the waiter.

I looked at him and sipped my wine.

"I want to work on this case," he said.

I set my glass down, thinking I had misheard him.

"You already worked on it."

"For two months. I want to see it concluded," he said.

I was not prepared for this conversation. I felt a little odd talking to Peter Connolly about forming an alliance to work this or any case together. I wanted to cut the conversation short.

"I'm not getting paid for this, Peter. I never asked Collier for money."

"What's that mean? You think I'm looking for a payday?" he said, leaning over the table.

"I don't know. All I know is that you have a reputation for being a little unpredictable."

"Really? You're the one who got busted off the job for being a drunk. I have never shown up anywhere drunk. So, who is the unpredictable one."

I took another sip of wine. Stalling. It was true, they had run off the job for being drunk, and I also took a swing at my sergeant. Who at that time was Webster. That was the reason for our tension. I couldn't argue with the truth of what Connolly said.

"How's your relationship with Webster?"

"I'm sure better than yours. Look, the two of us together are better than apart. Right? Something is not right with this missing kid," he said, leaning back in his chair.

"Meaning you suspect something and want to follow it."

"I have no idea what happened to that girl. But I do know I only had two months on the case and no new information. It doesn't sit right."

I could only nod my head. How did my life get so messed up that I was now partnering with Peter Connolly?

# 21

After leaving Connolly, I drove to Sarah Collier's apartment. I knocked twice before she let me in.

Briefly, I explained about Connolly and what that meant for the search for the truth about her sister.

She only nodded as she poured herself a drink and then poured one for me. I accepted the glass and took a long drink.

She sat down heavily on the couch, looked at me, and started crying. She cried for a solid five minutes. Then she shook it off as if it had never happened.

"What's the plan for you two super sleuths?"

"I still have questions I need answered before I tell my plans. I'm sure Pete feels the same."

"He didn't find out a whole lot last time," she said.

I was confused by her reaction. I figured she would like the fact that two people were working on the case. Even though one was a washed-up alcoholic and the other one was Peter Connolly.

"He's agreed to help on this without charge."

She nodded, remaining silent.

I had hoped she would be happy that two highly trained investigators would be looking into her case. But then I remembered it was me and Pete Connolly. I would have been crying too.

She looked up at me and hunched her shoulders tight to her neck.

"I feel like I have been a fool," she said.

I sat beside her; my drink forgotten.

"How so?"

"Looking into my sister's disappearance. All the time and money wasted. Chasing a suspect who isn't a suspect."

She looked down at the floor.

"Need any more reasons?"

I placed my glass on the coffee table. Took her hand in mine and held it.

"You're doing what you think you should. Someone made your sister disappear."

She nodded, squeezing my hand.

"I know. And whoever it is has been out there free all this time. Do you really think anything will change that? Even the dynamic duo of Connolly and Langley?"

I said nothing, mainly because I could think of nothing to say that would not affirm her thoughts. There was nothing new to this case. Her sister was gone and whoever the guilty party was, had gotten away with it.

"Why didn't you tell me your mother paid for Connolly?"

She leaned her head against my shoulder. The smell of alcohol was strong as she sighed.

"I was embarrassed. And mom told me not to ever tell or my dad would find out."

"Why would your dad be mad?"

"I don't know."

We were silent then. Neither of us said anything that would break the connection we had. The heat from her body felt good to me.

## 22

The next morning, I awoke on the couch in my office. I had only a vague memory of getting here. After I had left Sarah, I went to the Clover Leaf and drank way too much once again.

I sat up on the couch. My head was foggy but not as bad as some mornings. I needed to make

some progress on this case, or I needed to let it go. I really had no clues with which to work. And Pete Connolly had no idea where to start, either.

One thing we did agree on was Sarah Collier had issues that we had only begun to discover.

I made myself some coffee and was pouring the first cup when the door

opened and Kim came walking in. She gave me a quick glance, looking around the room, then shook her head. How many times had she seen me hungover, half drunk, or even worse, fully drunk in this office?

I felt a slight pang of guilt as I saw the look on her face. Disgust or disappointment, I couldn't tell. She said nothing as she came in and took her seat at her desk. She looked fresh and well-groomed, and I was still in last night's clothes, smelling like a brewery, and feeling like hell.

"You get anywhere with Collier last night?" Kim said as she sat down.

"No."

"Case wise I mean."

"Funny." I took a sip of coffee. "She is a strange woman. She is one of the few people that make me feel like a lightweight in the drinking department," I said, pouring Kim a cup of coffee.

"Well, she seems to be a unique person."

"Unique?"

I gave Kim her cup and sat down at my desk and dug some eye drops from the drawer.

"You can't keep doing what you're doing, Joe."

"What am I doing?"

"Drinking too much, not keeping on top of what your job is, and you're slipping to the bottom of the pile when it comes to private investigators." She looked straight at me as she spoke, watching me put the drops in my eyes and blink several times.

"How do you figure that?"

She made a noise in her throat that I took for scoffing. Kim scoffed a lot at me over the years. It was one of her most annoying habits, but also one of the reasons I trusted her opinion over others.

"I dug into Sarah as much as I could. Her life is a mess. Job hopping, skipping out on debts. Her parents seem to bail her out when she gets too far over her head."

"Well, maybe she hasn't made the best choices in life. I don't know."

"You do remember you're partnered with Peter Connolly."

I did remember that. I sipped my coffee and thought about my life choices.

## 23

I called Connolly and asked for a meeting at noon at a little seafood place I liked down by the beach.

He came to the table and sat down without preamble. He was dressed, as always, near flawlessly. He had a nice button-down shirt with sleeves rolled up and slacks that were creased sharp enough to slice the humidity hanging in the air.

"You look like hell, Joey," he said, removing his two-hundred-dollar sunshades and smiling.

"We need a game plan for this case. It is a big nothing so far," I said, ignoring his witty repartee.

"It was a big nothing from the start when it was mine and everyone else's. There are no clues or trails to follow."

"Sarah insists that something is there. And there is a missing girl."

"Missing for a long time with no clue as to where or why."

I sat there not knowing what to say, trying to figure out in my head how to approach a case that was ice cold.

We ordered our food, and as the waitress walked away, Peter looked at me and said,

"No cocktail or booze for lunch?"

I shook my head.

"I need to keep clear-headed to work on this case."

Peter laughed, a short laugh, more like a snort than a laugh. I was already annoyed with him.

"Not like you to pass up an opportunity to have a drink."

I wanted a drink. I also wanted to punch Peter in the face. Both would have to wait.

The waitress sat our food in front of us and asked if there was anything else she could get us. Peter made an embarrassing attempt to get her phone number, and she acted like it flattered her. I just wanted to eat.

We ate in silence, each lost in our own thoughts on what to do with the information we had, or more precisely, the information we didn't have.

Peter looked up and put his fork down hard.

"We are damn fools, Joey."

"I know. But tell me why you think so."

"Instead of looking at this case by going to the family and trying to kick rocks. We should start with the kids."

"The kids?" I said, chewing a bite of food.

"Her friends."

"I doubt any of them are still around."

"We talk with Diana's friends," he said, as if I had said nothing. "Then we go to the police and see if there are any other similar cases."

"Other missing kids from that time frame. Not a bad idea. I'm not exactly welcomed at the castle."

"I'll handle the police side. You try to track her friends down. Some must still be on the island."

The idea wasn't a terrible one, I'll admit. Because it was Peter's idea, I was reluctant. I still wanted to punch him in the face.

# 24

We left the restaurant, each with a job to do. Connolly was going to the police department to talk about other missing kids. I was heading to Sarah's apartment.

She wasn't home. I had no idea where she'd be at this time of day, so I went looking. There was a bar around the corner from her apartment. I had a hunch she would be there. My hunch was right.

She was sitting at a table alone, a drink in front of her. The bar smelled of stale cigarette smoke, old booze, and body odor. My shoes made sticky sounds as I walked across the room to her table.

She looked up when she saw me and smiled. "Need a drink?" she said, pointing to a chair.

I sat down as she motioned to the bartender. The waitress brought two drinks. I downed mine in a single drink.

"Are you OK?" I asked, motioning for another drink.

She nodded, then shrugged her shoulders. She looked at me and smiled.

"I think so. I'm alive, Diana isn't."

I had nothing to say to that. She waited until the waitress delivered our drinks, then said,

"I think I'm being followed."

I looked around the bar. The few people in here didn't seem to pay her any mind. They all appeared to be fighting demons of their own.

"Who? Where?"

"Not in here. He followed me from my apartment. I don't know who. A man."

Her words were slurred, and she had trouble looking at me. I wondered how much she'd had to drink so far.

"Why would they follow you?"

"Maybe I'm crazy. They may have just been going the same way I was."

She sat up straight in her chair and took a deep breath.

"Can you take me home?"

"I walked here. Can you walk?"

"If you help me," she said, standing and giggling at the same time.

She placed her hand on the table to balance herself. I stood watching her, not offering help.

We went outside and headed for her apartment. She took my arm, holding it close to her body. She said nothing else about being followed, but I kept watch as we walked to see if I could see anyone.

Inside the apartment, Sarah offered me a drink. I accepted. We sat next to each other on her old couch, sipping our drinks. She caught me looking at her and smiled.

"This is nice," she said.

She leaned toward me and kissed me. It was a warm soft kiss, her lips wet from the scotch. I kissed her, then pulled away.

"I need to go."

I set my glass down and reluctantly left the apartment. She sat watching me, not saying anything.

# 25

As I drove back to my office, I was hoping Connolly had made more progress than I had. I didn't even ask Sarah about Diana's friends. I kept thinking about the kiss, though.

I had refused to take advantage of Sarah in her condition. Which took more self-will than I had ever shown before.

Kim was gone for the day, which was good for me. I didn't want her asking questions or judging my actions. I found the note she left on my desk.

A message to call Peter and a cell phone number. I picked up the office phone and dialed, hoping for good news.

"Any luck?" he asked when he answered.

"She was in no condition to talk."

"I guess you have to catch her early."

Ignoring his attempt at humor, I said,

"You find anything?"

"Some names Webster gave me of some friends Diana had back then."

"What do you want to do with it?"

"Meet in the morning. I'm going home."

The phone clicked, then silence. If he was going home, I was going to go have a drink or two.

As I walked to the Clover Leaf, I was thinking along the way. The drinks I'd had when I was with Sarah were wearing off.

When I stepped up on the sidewalk half a block from the bar, I could see the light from the open sign glowing in the window, casting a red shadow on the sidewalk. It would soon be pitch dark.

Hands grabbed me from behind, shoving me into the alley. Someone pushed me from behind, causing me to hit my head on the cement wall. I tried to turn.

A fist hammered my kidneys. I cried out in pain. Another set of hands was pushing my head into the wall.

"Don't look at us. You keep your head turned."

I didn't recognize the voice. He grabbed my hair, pulled my head back, and slammed it into the wall. I felt the skin rip and blood flowing from my forehead.

Someone kicked my leg in the bend of the knee. I fell in a heap, hitting my face on the ground. Both men began kicking my ribs and stomach. I tried screaming but couldn't get enough breath to make any sound.

From the corner of my eye that wasn't swelling shut, I saw a flash of white tennis shoe. It hit me in the head. The man kept kicking me in the head.

He stopped kicking me in the head long enough to say,

"You better leave the missing girl missing or we will be back."

He kicked me once more in the head. I saw a flash of brightness for a moment and my body relaxed. That was the last thing I remembered.

# 26

The name badge on her shirt said Astrid F. BSN. It was in my face as she stood in front of me, dabbing my forehead with an alcohol swab. I flinched when she applied pressure, causing her to make soothing sounds. I sat on the edge of the bed in the E.R. and held my side with my arm.

The curtain pushed back, and the doctor came in with a folder in his hand. He handed the folder to Astrid F. BSN, then looked at me and said,

"Ribs aren't broken, but you may be sore for a few days. You may be concussed. You'll have a black eye for a while. I'd advise taking it easy for a few days. If something changes, come back."

He left the room without waiting for me to reply. His bedside manner was not to my liking, but I let it slide. I had bigger problems than a snooty doctor.

Out in the hallway, I heard a familiar voice talking with the nurses. I glanced up at the nurse.

"I'd be grateful if you told that cop out there, I'm in a coma."

She only grinned. I figured she'd be no help to me. The curtain pulled back again as Captain Webster came into the small room.

He had a look of amusement on his face.

"I heard some drunk got rolled outside the Leaf. I knew it was you."

"Isn't a mugging above a captain's pay grade?"

"In most cases. What did you see?"

I glanced over at him as the nurse stepped back.

"Nothing. It was too fast. Two men and a white sneaker."

"You were drunk."

"I wasn't."

"BAC is above the limit, not much, but enough. Nurses say they smelled booze on you."

I looked up at Astrid. She only shrugged as she placed a bandage on my forehead. She pressed it in place. I flinched back.

"I don't know who did this. I have never had problems at the bar before. It has to be the case."

"A twenty plus year old case? I know you're drunk now."

Webster stepped in front of me so I could see him.

"You look like you'll live."

"What are we going to do about this?"

Webster stepped around the nurse to the curtain. He looked at me, then at his notes.

"Two men, white shoes. I'll put an all points out now."

I was thinking of a reply, but he left the room. Webster had come to gloat at me being injured. But drinking or not, I recalled the words one of the men said to me and I knew this attack was because of the Collier case.

# 27

It was late when I left the E.R. I drove home needing rest and a drink. I pulled to the curb and cut the engine. Looking in the shadows for potential muggers. I saw nothing.

As I unlocked the door to the staircase, a shoe scrapped behind me. I turned, startled, and drew my arm back to punch. It was Sarah. I relaxed a little.

"What are you doing here?"

"I heard what happened. I came to check on you. Are you all right?"

I unlocked the door and stepped aside so she could go up first. I climbed slowly behind her. The exertion made my ribs hurt and caused me to breathe hard.

"How'd you hear about it?"

"Bartender at the Clover Leaf. I went there to find you."

Word must have traveled fast inside the bar. It was embarrassing to think about. Inside my apartment, I offered her a drink as I poured one for myself. She refused. I looked at her as I sipped.

"I came here to say I'm sorry I ran you away like that."

"You didn't run me away. I was thinking of you."

"Me? How?"

I shook my head.

"It doesn't matter now. You shouldn't be out." I pointed to my face. "This happened because of this case."

She stared at me. I said,

"One of the two men who attacked me said to leave the missing girl missing. Or something like that."

"I don't understand. Who would do that?"

"I don't know. But earlier I wanted to ask about Diana's friends. Can you give me some who may still be around?"

"Of course, but what do her friends have to do with any of this?"

I shrugged. I had no answers. Only questions and a hurting head.

"Can I stay here tonight?"

I looked at her. She smiled at me. I wanted her, but I needed to be strong. I stepped toward her as she stepped closer to me.

She kissed me. Soft and slow at first, then harder and full of passion. I responded the only way a man knows how. I kissed her back just as hard.

She broke the embrace and smiled at me.

"I want you, please," she said.

I wanted her too. And against my better judgment, I led her to the bedroom. My ribs didn't hurt as much as they did before.

# 28

The sun shone through the window. I squinted my eyes against the glare. My body felt like one large bruise. It ached and hurt every time I moved. My left eye felt like it was almost swollen shut, my vision was a sliver of what it should be.

She moved next to me, snuggling closer, her back to me. A slim back with ribs showing. Her hair was all matted and balled on the pillow.

I hadn't had as much restraint as I thought. Sarah had come here, knowing what she wanted from me. Why did I feel guilty about it?

I sat up on the edge of the bed. I gasped lightly and pressed my hand into my ribs. Sarah rolled over. Our eyes met as she blinked to wake up.

"Morning," she said, stretching.

The sheet slid down, exposing her breast. I reached over and covered her. She giggled.

"Last night you wanted to see them."

"Last night shouldn't have happened."

Sarah sat up, the sheet falling. Her nakedness was a temptation I didn't need this morning. I stood as she said,

"Are you saying it was a mistake being with me?"

"Not for the reason you may think, but yeah."

I pulled my pants on slowly.

"I don't think it was. We are adults, after all."

"You're a client. And I..."

My words trailed off when I realized they sounded hollow to my own ears. They must have sounded condescending to her.

"Don't kid yourself. I'm a full grown woman capable of making my own decisions."

Not wanting to argue, I changed the subject and continued getting dressed.

"You were going to tell me about Diana's friends."

She got out of the bed and gathered her clothes. She put her bra on as she said,

"The only one I know that is still on the island is Emily Franklin. That was her maiden name, anyway."

"How do I find her?"

Her pants went on next.

"I don't know. She was a janitor at the motel on Sea Line last I knew."

"I have to meet Peter Connolly this morning. Maybe he has more information to follow up on."

She pulled her shirt over her head, then mussed her hair, trying to straighten it out.

"I'll be at my apartment rethinking my decisions."

She walked from the bedroom. The front door slammed a few seconds later. I had not wanted to make her angry, but I had. It would be best if what happened last night never happened again. I looked at the clock by the bed for the time.

# 29

Peter Connolly grimaced and stood from behind his desk when I walked in.

"What happened to you?"

He came around the desk, helped ease me into a chair. I was feeling helpless, and I hated that feeling.

"Had a problem last night. I don't know who did this, but I know it's related to this case."

I told him about last night's events up to Webster being a pain in the ass. I left out everything that had happened after leaving the hospital.

"That makes no sense. Who would care about a twenty something year old case that has had other eyes on it?"

I shrugged my shoulder. Even that hurt. I had a prescription they gave me last night for pain killers to fill at the pharmacy. I had my own way of killing pain. I couldn't wait for this meeting to be done so I could get on with it.

"Two men, you say? How old? White, black?"

"I don't know. How did you come on the names?"

"I split the six names between our girls."

Meaning Kim and his secretary. I nodded. Kim would probably find more than two old guys like us, anyway.

"I need to check out an Emily Franklin. She was a name Sarah gave me this morning."

"You've met her already this morning," he said, looking up from his calendar.

"I need to go," I said, standing.

Connolly watched me struggle to my feet. As I was catching my breath, he said,

"Try not to sleep with the client anymore."

I nodded as I turned to leave. There were a lot of motels on Sea Line. And Emily Franklin might not work at any of them.

# 30

There were eleven motels on Sea Line. After two hours of checking all of them, all I had was a sore back and ribs and no Emily Franklin.

She had worked at two of the motels in the past but quit a long time ago. I had a last known address. I drove to the area of town that was known locally as Welfare City. It was a poor area of town where all the island's poor migrated to. Hispanics, blacks, whites, even some other nationalities all huddled in Welfare City when dreams of island life crashed like a rogue wave over a surfer in the ocean.

The address I was looking for belonged to a small trailer house, what used to be called mobile homes. Though this one didn't look too mobile to me. Cinder blocks held one end of the house up. It didn't look too stable.

I knocked on the door and waited. I could smell animal feces. And urine, which I hoped was animal.

Several knocks later, a woman answered the door. Unless I missed my guess, she was too old to be Diana's age.

"Emily Franklin? I was told this was her address."

"Was. Not anymore. Who are you?"

I smiled what I hoped was a disarming smile, though with my black eye and bandage on my forehead, it felt sinister.

"Who are you, ma'am?"

She laughed at me. A smoker's laugh, phlegmy and rough. She had to be about sixty, though she could have been ninety.

"Ma'am. You're sucking up for something. I'm Rita Franklin. Emily's mother."

Thinking I was making progress, I said,

"Is Emily available to talk to?"

"No. Not for a while. She died a few years ago."

She stepped out onto the wood deck that served as a porch, closing the door behind her.

"What do you need with Emily? Why are you here?"

I stepped back involuntarily to avoid inhaling the body odor that floated off Rita Franklin.

"I wanted to talk to her about an old friend of hers. Diana Collier."

"I don't want to hear that name, mister. That girl is the reason my Emily is dead."

"My name is Joe Langley. I'm a P.I. looking into the case. What do you mean, she's the reason?"

"I ain't talking about this with you or no one else. Leave Mr. Langley, now."

She went into the house, closing the door before I could say anything else. I needed a drink and some quiet time.

# 31

My pickup was parked on the beach with the tailgate facing the water. I sat on the tailgate, watching the waves lap the sand beneath my bare feet. Bottles weren't allowed on the beach, but I twisted the cap off my beer and tossed it into the bed behind me. I took a long sip. The eight I'd already drunk earlier were starting to work.

Summer was ending. The people on the beach were trying to make the most of the time left. Swimmers splashed and played, kids and adults built sandcastles, and folks hid from the hot sun under umbrellas and canopies. As I watched the people on the beach doing typical tourist things, I was convinced that folks who fed the seagulls should be permanently banned from every beach in the country.

"Hey, how are you doing?" she said, startling me a bit.

Kim was standing next to the tailgate. She had walked up to me without me knowing. I made a mental note to be more watchful.

"I'm OK," I said, sipping my beer.

"How's the drinking going?"

"It's fine. What are you doing here?"

"I heard about last night. Wondering why you didn't call me."

She stepped around the truck bed to sit beside me on the tailgate.

"I got jumped. It's no big deal."

"You could have died."

I changed the subject.

"I asked Sarah about a friend of Diana's. She's dead. Her mom flipped when I showed up at her house asking questions."

"She was probably scared given the way you look," Kim said, nudging my arm with her shoulder as she sat beside me.

"What the hell am I doing? Nothing in this case makes sense. I feel I'm chasing my tail and gaining nothing."

"Maybe it's just a mystery, you know. At least you haven't slept with the client."

I looked over at her to see if she was smiling. She looked back at me and frowned.

"You slept with her, didn't you? Jesus, Joe."

"I know, I know," I said, swallowing the rest of my beer.

I got another bottle from the cooler behind me. I didn't offer Kim one. She would have refused anyway.

"This is why I quit working for you. You have no boundaries."

There was no arguing with the truth, so I didn't.

"You got a list of names from Connolly?"

"The information is at the office. I wanted to check on you. I knew you'd be out here or at the Leaf. I was worried."

"Worried even though you don't like me, huh?"

Kim got off the tailgate, walking a few steps toward her car. She turned back to me and said,

"Just because I don't like you, Joe, doesn't mean I don't love you."

She left me sitting there feeling worse about my misstep with Sarah. Maybe seagull feeders weren't the only ones who needed to be banned from the beach.

# 32

I drove to Connolly's office. I was desperate for any information that could help with this case. Connolly was in his office, a phone stuck to his ear when his secretary led me in. He motioned me to a chair in front of his desk. I sat and waited.

He hung up the phone and looked at me.

"I smell beer."

"Yes, you do. Any news I need to know about?"

He looked at me for a moment, then motioned to the phone.

"That was Webster. Telling me no one saw anything outside the bar last night."

"Figures. I didn't even see anything, and I had the best view."

"The point is, the police think it was random. Not connected to the case."

"I know what the man said as he was hitting me. What about the names?"

"Dead end. Only had two names. Both families moved off the island after the disappearance."

I told him about Emily Franklin and my encounter with her mother. He listened without comment until I finished.

"Dead ends everywhere."

I nodded, feeling at odds. He looked at me, then stood and said,

"Let's go for a ride."

I stood to follow.

"Ride where?"

"I'll drive. I don't know how much you've had, but I know how much I haven't."

He led the way from his office as I followed like a chastised child. His Lexus was way nicer than my old Ford. I felt out of place riding in it.

We drove to the scene of the crime. The neighborhood Diana had gone missing from.

Connolly didn't stop. He just kept driving in circles, block after block, looking at the houses in the neighborhood.

He pulled to the curb after about five trips around the area.

"We need to question more people. This time we need to ask the proper questions," he said, staring out the windshield.

I looked at him.

"More questions? This case has more questions than we can answer."

"Yeah, but those questions aren't the ones we should be asking."

It was my turn to stare out the window.

"OK. Where do we start this new approach?"

"Where each of us has started with this case. Ralph Norris."

I looked at him again. He put the car in gear, and we drove back to his office in silence. I tried to figure out what he was thinking but gave up. I saw no reason to talk to Norris again.

When he dropped me off at my truck, I headed to Sarah's apartment. I needed to talk to her about a lot of things. Mostly about what had happened between us the night before.

# 33

Sarah answered her door, drink in her hand. Her T-shirt was loose and not long enough to hide the black panties she wore underneath.

She invited me in and offered me a drink, which I accepted. I held my glass in my hand as she looked at me, sipping her drink.

"What do you want now? To insult me more? To tell me that the decisions I want to make are wrong?"

I drank my drink in one swallow.

"No, none of that. I wanted to tell you, I'm sorry."

She looked at me, surprised.

"Really?"

Nodding my head, I walked to the couch and sat. She came and sat beside me, placing a hand on my arm. My skin burned from the light contact.

"I'm sorry, I reacted like a little girl, too. I..."

I leaned in and kissed her. Once. I sat my glass on the coffee table as she adjusted her place on the couch. Pulling her knees under her, she placed her hands on my face and kissed me hard.

She aroused feelings in me I hadn't felt in a long time. Feelings I tried to fight off when they came over me. I didn't fight now. I surrendered completely to them.

Afterward, she lay in my arms in the bed, her head on my chest. My ribs screamed in protest when she moved, I said nothing that would break the contact. She ran the fingers of one hand through my chest hair as I stroked her hair.

After a while, I said,

"When was the last time you saw Emily Franklin?"

Her fingers stopped moving. She raised her head to look at me.

"God, years, I guess. Did you find her? How is she?"

"She's dead."

Sarah sat up on her elbow, looking at me.

"What?"

"I talked to her mother. She's a salty one. Said Emily died years ago. She said Diana was the reason for her death."

"Diana? How does she figure that?"

"I don't know. She wasn't exactly raring to talk to me about it. What do you think she meant?" Sarah sat up on her knees, pulling the blanket off both of us. Her nakedness excited me. She ran a hand through her hair.

"I have no idea. We were all kids when Diana disappeared."

I sat up on the bed, moving slowly to avoid as much pain as I could.

I looked over my shoulder at her.

"What do you know of the mom?"

"I don't remember the mother. I was older than Diana was, so I didn't hang out with her friends."

I stood and gathered my clothes. Sarah sighed as she got off the bed and began dressing.

"One thing about this," I said, pointing to the bed. "Everyone will hate this while I'm working this case."

She looked at the bed, then winked at me. I felt my blood pulse in my veins.

# 34

Back at my apartment, I took a shower. I got a half-full bottle of Chivas down from the cabinet and made myself a strong drink. I sat in my chair and stared out the window.

It was dark outside. Another day I felt was wasted. No answers, just more questions. I sipped my drink.

The ringing phone broke my mood. I picked up the handset.

"Joe. Get to the office now."

Kim's voice made me sit up in my chair.

"What's wrong?"

"Just get here fast."

There were cop cars parked in front of my building, flashing lights bouncing a red and blue strobe of shadows off the bakery windows and the buildings along the street. I parked behind a patrol car.

The bottom door was smashed in. Upstairs, my office door had been kicked in, the jamb split where the lock had been. Kim stood surrounded by two uniformed officers I didn't know. Other officers were looking around the office in different locations.

The office was a mess. Papers strewn everywhere. The one file cabinet I had was turned over, the contents were scattered on the floor. Pictures lay in broken frames on the floor. Both desks had been rifled through.

"What happened?" I asked, walking up to Kim.

She gave me a hug, the two uniforms staring at us.

"Joe, look what they did."

I broke the embrace, holding her at arm's length.

"Were you here? Are you OK?"

She shook her head.

"I'm fine. I got a call from the police officers when they found the door downstairs unlocked."

A young officer with a name tag that read Jameson said,

"Dispatch called her. We thought you were in here drunk again and forgot to lock the door. We found this when we got up here."

I gave Officer Jameson what I hoped was a withering look. He seemed not to notice. He was young, mid-twenties. His blonde hair cut high and tight.

"Any ideas who did this?" I asked him.

"It's your office, Langley. Who have you pissed off lately?"

"Do we know each other, Officer?" I said, turning to face him straight on.

"We've never met. But I heard about you."

"Then you should know I'm a sonofabitch."

I faced the room. Cops were watching me as I spoke to Jameson.

"Everyone out. I don't need your help. Get out."

Officer Jameson looked at me, then shrugged. He led the others out of the office.

# 35

Kim and I spent the next several hours cleaning the mess up. We talked about the things that had happened since taking on the Collier case. It was a lot to process.

Kim was straightening papers on her desk, putting things back in order. I was trying to decide if I needed everything that had been scattered off mine.

"It's missing," Kim said, holding a folder in each hand.

"What's missing?"

I threw a handful of paper in the trash can by my knee.

"The information I had on the friends. It's gone."

"Why would they break into an office and steal paperwork that can be replaced in minutes?"

"Why would they attack you in the alley?" she said, throwing the empty folders on the floor.

"Was there anything useful in the file?"

Kim shook her head.

"No. Not really. Only a couple of names that I got from Connolly. Dead ends mostly."

She looked at her desk for a moment, then at me.

"The one name in the file that jumped at me was Rita...I can't remember her last name."

"Franklin? What about her?"

"Rita Franklin. Her daughter is dead, too."

I told Kim about my visit with Rita Franklin earlier that day. She listened to my opinion of the woman, which wasn't much.

"She hasn't always lived in that part of town."

That meant nothing to me. Kim waited for me to catch on to what she meant. When I didn't, she pulled her chair over by mine and sat down.

"If Emily Franklin was friends with Diana Collier, where did they live, Joe?"

I looked at her. She was watching me.

"I need to find the old house over in the Collier neighborhood."

Kim nodded and patted my leg like I had answered a test question correctly. She looked around at the rest of the mess that was left.

"You think Connolly got hit?"

That was a good question. It would make sense to break into both offices. I told her I didn't know.

"I'll call him and tell him to check," Kim said, reaching for the phone on my desk.

Though I could only hear one side of the conversation, Kim's tone changed from conversational to concern. She hung up the phone and looked at me.

"We need to go over there."

She stood, heading for the door.

"Did someone break into his, too?" I asked, following her out the door, not closing it.

"Worse."

She said nothing else as we drove to Pete Connolly's office.

# 36

The flames could be seen for blocks. Firetrucks were everywhere, firemen in full bunker gear working hard to fight the blaze that engulfed the building.

Kim parked her car in a no parking zone. We got out and stood with the other onlookers standing behind the yellow tape area watching the firefighters fight the blaze. One of the onlookers was Peter Connolly.

We moved to stand beside him. He was watching his office building go up in flames, pieces of wall fell to the ground as the firemen retreated a safe distance.

He noticed us standing next to him.

"All gone. Everything I have worked for is all gone."

I looked over at Kim.

"This is no coincidence."

Tears welled in his eyes as he looked at me. The lights from the firetrucks and police cars reflected off his eyes giving them a glassy look.

"Joe, Kim. Thanks for coming down to see the end of my world."

"I'm so sorry, Peter," Kim said, rubbing his shoulder.

"I got broke into tonight, you get torched. What do you think the odds are it being a lark?"

"You got burgled?"

"They took the notes Kim had prepared from the names you gave her."

He looked at the fire, which was now mostly smoke as the firefighters had the flames out.

"I guess they did the same here, too."

I sent Kim home. The next few hours I stood with my old nemesis, now partner, and watched the cleanup of the fire. There were a few firemen mopping up in the ruins of the building.

The interior of the building was completely gone, all that was left was a shell of the exterior, now blackened with smoke and soot. Water puddled in the street up to the ankles in some places.

A fireman in yellow bunker gear came up to us. His helmet had an emblem with the words Lieutenant across it.

"Are you Mr. Connolly?" he said, looking at Pete.

Pete nodded. The Lieutenant turned to face the building, pointing as he talked.

"Sorry about your building. It's too hot inside to look for a cause right now. But it seems to be in the parking area underneath. What little I could see indicates the fire moved upward."

He spat. A dark, sooty looking mess that splatted the sidewalk.

"What concerns me is the building itself. It's unstable. The city is going to have a crew here to knock these walls down. We can get in there when it cools off some."

Pete said nothing to the fireman. My words didn't seem appropriate enough. I stood there watching the men work. Wondering what shoe would drop next.

# 37

After a late night and a long day, I was going to go home. I left Peter with a promise to meet in the morning at my office and team up. I was worried about Sarah. She was more involved in this case than anyone, which meant she was in more danger. I drove to her place instead.

She let me in, asking why I smelled like smoke. I explained everything that had happened. She listened, her drink half empty, forgotten on the counter.

"You think I'm in danger?"

"I do. I don't know how much, yet."

"Why now? After all this time, I mean."

"I don't think this is recent. I have a hunch, but I'm keeping it to myself."

"You want a drink?" she said, picking her glass up.

I shook my head. She smiled.

"You want something else?"

I nodded. She led me to the bedroom where I worked out all my frustrations.

The next morning, I met Peter as planned. I had showered and washed my clothes at Sarah's, so although I wore the same thing from last night, they were clean. Which was more than I could say for Peter Connolly.

He still had the same button-down shirt and tan slacks from the night before. They smelled of smoke and sweat. He looked as if he hadn't slept. His hair, usually so neatly combed, was awry and wild.

He began talking as soon as I got in his car.

"Our first stop is Ralph Norris. He better be cooperative."

"What are we talking to him again for?"

"For answers," he said, shifting into gear and pulling away from the curb.

"Well, that clears that up."

"Joe, Norris lived in that neighborhood. He saw the kids almost every day. Even if he didn't interact with them, he saw them. Remember, before they discovered he was a," he made air quotes, "perv, he was a neighbor, and a trusted guy."

"OK. You think he remembers kids from nearly three decades ago?"

"It's worth asking."

I got lost in my thoughts as we drove along. If Pete wanted to ask questions, maybe I should ask some of my own.

# 38

Ralph Norris' yard and house looked the way I remembered it looking. We got out and walked to the front door. Pete knocked. I stood next to him patiently.

A woman answered the door. She was older than the picture I had seen her in before, but still an attractive woman. Mrs. Norris.

As Peter introduced us, I could see her facial expression change from friendly to guarded.

"Your husband spoke with me before, ma'am. Did he tell you that?" I said.

She nodded her head, her short hair moving little with the motion.

"You're the one who thinks he's innocent?" "We both do," Peter said, smiling.

I didn't smile. My face still looked like a pieced together monster collage. My eye was less swollen, but still bruised.

She opened the door wider, stepping aside to let us in.

"I'm Sharon. Come on in. We are in the kitchen having coffee."

Peter followed Sharon. I followed Peter. She led us both to a large kitchen dining room combination. Ralph sat drinking coffee watching ESPN. He saw us behind his wife and muted the sound.

"Gentleman, how can I help you? Mr. Langley, I'm surprised to see you so soon."

He remained seated. Sharon sat in a chair to his right. Pete and I remained standing.

Since this was his idea, I let Peter lead the way.

"Mr. Norris, I'm Peter Connolly. I don't know if you remember me."

"I remember you. You were an asshole the last time you were in my house."

I chuckled lightly. Peter had made his usual impression on the man. Peter looked at me, then back to Norris and said,

"Well, Mr. Langley thinks you're innocent. I agree with him. We have some questions about the neighborhood we'd like to ask."

"I haven't been in that neighborhood in years. Not since they..."

I interrupted.

"We want to ask about some of the kids. Diana's friends, surcly you saw them a lot if you saw Diana almost daily."

He looked at his wife, who was looking at the table in front of her, not meeting his eyes.

"OK. If I can be of help."

"How many other kids did Diana usually go to the courts with?" Peter asked.

Norris stared at the man, then shrugged.

"I have no idea."

"Did you know Ben and Marie Collier?"

"Only to say hi to. They were big deals in the city. He was always doing real estate deals. We read about it in the papers all the time."

"Did you know a Rita Franklin?"

Sharon looked up from the table, her eyes locked on me. I looked at her and said,

"Do you know that name?"

She stared at me a bit longer, then nodded her head.

"Her daughter died a few years ago."

"Yeah, that's right."

"Killed is the rumor the sister likes to tell."

I stepped forward.

"Rita has a sister?"

Sharon shook her head.

"Not Rita, Emily. She works at the hospital. Her name is Astrid Franklin."

I looked over at Peter. I turned and walked out of the kitchen. Peter, confused, followed me.

# 39

I sat in Peter's car waiting for him. When he got in, he stared over at me.

"What's wrong with you?"

"Astrid F. BSN," I said, as if that would explain everything.

"OK," he said, like he understood.

Peter started the car and put his seat belt on. He put the car in gear and, as he pulled out from the curb, he said,

"Where to now?"

"Hospital. I need to see my nurse."

I could see him shake his head, but he didn't say anything. I figured now was a good time to break the news.

"Me and Sarah. We're sleeping together."

He glanced over at me.

"Not the best way to avoid conflict, sleeping with a client. Even one that isn't paying. I wonder what the state would say if they knew?"

"We know what they would say, and I don't care. She and I are alike in so many ways."

"I can think of one."

I looked over at him. He was staring out the windshield, the picture of innocence.

"Not the drinking. Beyond that. It's more than that."

He said nothing more, and we soon pulled into the hospital parking lot. As he looked for a place to park, I said,

"Just drop me off. I'll catch a ride back."

"You don't want me going with you?"

I opened the door and got out, letting the door close as I walked toward the doubled door entrance.

I asked the desk receptionist for Astrid Franklin. She directed me toward the E.R. doors.

Stepping through the doors, I stepped into a world of sanitized cleanliness and the strong smell of antiseptic.

She was sitting behind the nurse's counter, working on the computer. She looked up as I stepped up to the counter.

"Can I help you, sir?"

She looked up, and she didn't recognize me.

"I need to talk to you, Astrid. If you have a moment."

"I don't. Do you need to see a doctor?" she said, looking at my face.

"Saw him already, along with you. I want to talk about your sister."

She rolled her chair back a bit, looking at me, curious.

"What about my sister?"

I pointed to my face and said,

"I think this is connected to her. Please, it won't take long."

She looked around the room. No one was watching us. She stood, came around the counter, and motioned for me to follow her.

# 40

She led me to a break room. A large table in the middle of the room offered plenty of chairs. I introduced myself as I took a seat in one, as she sat across from me.

"I visited your mom looking for Emily. She didn't seem to want to talk to me. How did it happen?"

Astrid shrugged her shoulders.

"I don't know, really. A car wreck, they say. But mom and I think it was murder."

"Any reason to think it was?"

"No," she shook her head. "My mom isn't well. If you talked to her, you know."

"Where did she live before she lived in welf...where she's living now?"

"Welfare City? You can say it, that's what the place is called. We lived over on Water View."

Water View was a nice area of town inside the Big Beach area. Expensive homes, nice cars, lots of money.

"Quite a ways from Water View to Welfare City."

"The street mom lives on is Rice, but I get what you mean. Emily died. Seems a few months later we moved. I got out, went to school and got a job here."

"How old are you?"

She smiled. I'm twenty-eight. Emily was older than me by a few years."

"Do you remember Diana Collier?"

She nodded.

"She got taken, and it changed everything."

"Taken? By whom? What do you know about her disappearing?"

"Those words all mean the same, Mr. Langley."

"They can."

She was silent, staring around the windowless room. Her shoulders slumped, and she said,

"I don't know about Diana. But mom insisted... insists that Emily was murdered because of what she knew about Diana's disappearance."

"Did she have any proof of that?"

"No. Just a dead daughter. Diana was older than Emily by a couple of years. Emily was older than me. I didn't hang around with them."

"How old was Emily when she died?"

"Twenty-two. She died ten years ago. Maybe it was an accident. Who would wait ten years to kill a person if it had anything to do with Diana?"

I didn't say anything. I was thinking it didn't sound so crazy anymore. Why wait twenty-two years to beat up a has been and burn the building of a man with alleged criminal connections?

# 41

I lay beside Sarah in my bed. She was snoring softly as I lay there, thinking about the day. I knew more than I did. I just couldn't fit the pieces together. I listened to Sarah breathing. I didn't care about anything except listening to her breathe right now.

I sat up slowly, my ribs still ached if I moved too fast. Catching my breath, I stood and walked naked to the kitchen. I poured myself a scotch and got a cube of ice from the freezer. The booze tasted good, but I needed food.

I checked my freezer. I had nothing but ice.

Sarah came from the bedroom, wrapped in the sheet. She was watching me. I poured her a drink and gave her the glass.

"What are you doing?"

"I'm hungry. I have no food here."

"I don't want to go out. We can order in."

The phone rang. I stared at it, hoping it would stop. It didn't. I picked up the phone and punched the talk button.

"Joe, I'm on my way to you. Meet me downstairs in four minutes. We got something to do."

As usual, Peter didn't waste time on pleasantries or give me a chance to say anything as he hung up.

I looked at Sarah.

"I gotta go. Order something if you want."

I passed her on my way to the bedroom and my clothes. I dressed in a hurry. Sarah stood watching me. She lay back down on the bed, the sheet still covering her.

"Just hurry back," she said, closing her eyes.

Not figuring it was appropriate, I didn't kiss her. I just left the apartment. When I got downstairs, Peter was waiting for me.

I got in the passenger seat. He sped away from the curb, driving faster than he should have in the dark.

"Where are we going?"

"Welfare City."

I felt my heart rate increase.

"Why?"

He ignored the question. Instead, he motioned to the back seat.

"Kim left her notes in your office. Now they're missing. Barbara took her notes home. She gave them to me when we were discussing the fire."

"OK," I said, not following his thoughts.

"What did you find out today?"

"Emily Franklin died ten years ago."

He nodded as if I had just imparted deep knowledge to him.

As fast as he drove, it didn't take long to make it to Rice Street and the tiny, run-down mobile home of Rita Franklin.

Police cars sat out front. The lights were off, nobody seemed to be in a hurry. One car was an unmarked unit. A detective car.

We got out and walked to the yellow tape that stretched across the small yard. I already knew what all this meant, but I was hoping I was wrong.

"Who's the detective on scene?" Pete asked a young cop standing by the tape.

"Captain Webster."

"Go get him, now."

The young cop stood there for a moment longer, looking at us, then turned and walked toward the small wooden porch that led to the front door.

He said something to Webster, who looked out at us. I thought I heard him cussing as he came down the wobbly steps and across the yard.

"What do you two want?" he said, stopping on his side of the tape.

"I heard the call on the scanner. What do you have here, Captain?"

"I'm waiting for a warrant to search the place. Rita Franklin is dead in her hallway."

"Heart attack?" Pete said.

"A bullet in her head."

I swore. Webster looked at me.

"I guess this isn't connected either, huh, Captain?" I said.

# 42

I sat in Peter's car, the air conditioner working overtime to find the heat and humidity in the air. Pete sat in the driver's seat next to me, watching the crime scene unfold.

"This sucks."

That was the understatement of the year, as far as I was concerned.

"It isn't good," I said.

Another understatement. Peter reached into the back seat and retrieved the file folder. Turning on the interior light, he opened it and fumbled through the papers.

I didn't know what he was looking for or how to help him. Instead, I said,

"If all these incidents are connected, then a lot of people are in danger."

Peter made a noise in his throat.

"We don't even know who could be doing all this. The same guy who twenty-two years ago took a fourteen year old girl. That makes no sense." "Unless the one who did it is getting worried and taking precautions."

"Worried about what?" he said, lifting a sheet of paper from the folder.

He handed it to me. I looked at it. A list of names.

"People we've talked to," I said.

He nodded.

"We need a new list with those names and where they lived twenty-two years ago."

"I know Rita Franklin used to live on Water View. Her daughter told me that."

"Same neighborhood as the missing girl," Pete said.

"Can we use your office?"

I shook my head.

"It's closed for repairs. My landlord won't let me use it until the doors get repaired. We can use my apartment."

He nodded, put the car in reverse, and left the scene. I felt I needed to warn him about my place.

"Sarah's at my place, just so you know."

He looked over at me and shrugged.

"With what we have going on, she may be safer there than in her own apartment. She should stay close until this is over."

I rode in silence. With what we knew, how many dots could we connect?

# 43

In my apartment, Peter spread his files on the small coffee table. Sarah got dressed and made coffee, which I didn't know I had. I watched them work. Peter picked up a tablet and pen. Across the first page of the legal pad, he wrote the official statement of investigations, 'What do we Know.'

"All right. What do we know? Let's go in order."

"I took the coffee cup Sarah offered me. She gave Pete a cup and then poured one for herself. She sat at the counter on a bar stool and listened to us.

"In order," I said. "We have a missing girl twenty-two years ago. An investigation that was big on promise but short on reality."

"OK," he said, writing down Diana Collier's name.

"The investigator was a man named Bob Reeves," I said.

"Where is he now?" Pete asked, writing his name down.

"Dead. Car wreck coming back from the Collier's, ten years ago."

Peter looked up at me. I stared back at him.

"Emily Franklin, dead, ten years ago. Car wreck," he wrote more on his tablet.

"Ralph Norris, a dead end everyone chased. Including the sister," I said, looking over at Sarah.

She still sat silent watching us.

"Not just the sister, but other investigators."

I nodded. For the next two hours we sat drinking a lot of coffee and talking about the case, and facts we knew. At the end, Peter had written four pages of notes. Names, dates, and events.

There was nothing tying them together. Just a bunch of names on a page. Pete held the pad up.

"Lots of information but nothing solid, like a lead. Who beat you up? Who burned my building down? Who killed Rita Franklin?"

"Emily's mother?" Sarah asked, sitting up straight on her stool.

I nodded, then pointed at Peter.

"What's landlord say about the insurance?" He laughed a humorless laugh, then shook his head.

"No insurance in effect. I had just bought the building and was waiting for underwriting."

"Damn, that's bad luck."

"That was a nice building. Who'd you buy it from?" Sarah asked.

"My old landlord. Mickey Holt."

I just stared at Peter, who looked over at me. "Mickey Holt owns my building."

"Good guy. Gave me a heck of a deal."

# 44

After Peter left my apartment, I sat on the couch and thought about what we had discussed. Sarah sat down next to me. She put her hand on my knee.

"I think I'm scared."

"You'll be OK. I won't let you out of my sight until this is over."

"I hope you're right. I like being in your sight."

She smiled at me. I smiled back, feeling foolish. The feeling disappeared when she kissed me. I responded to the kiss the way a man should. The next hour was a blur of exertion.

We lay in the dark next to each other. I had a feeling the investigation was going to go in a direction Sarah wouldn't like. I needed her assurance that she was willing to see this through.

"Are you sure you want us to keep digging?"

I felt her head nod against my chest.

"Yes. Whoever did all these things needs to be stopped before something worse happens."

"Four people are dead. That's pretty bad."

"Four?" she said, raising her head to look at me. "I count three. Emily, her mom, and the cop."

"Diana."

She laid her head back on my chest. The wetness of her tears was warm on my chest. I stroked her hair.

"I just always think of her as missing. I hate knowing she's dead and I may never find her."

"You had to have known it was never going to be a happy ending."

The nod again. A sniffle, wet from crying.

"I did. But I didn't. You know?"

I didn't know. I had never lost anyone to a violent crime. I was an only child, and my folks were still alive.

I didn't say anything. I just held her until we fell asleep.

The next morning, a knock on my door startled me. It was a banging. Constant, and hard.

I grabbed my clothes and dressed as I went to the door. I had no peephole. I opened the door. Kim pushed her way in as I opened the door.

"I got something to show you."

"Keep your voice down. Sarah is sleeping."

She handed me a piece of paper and said,

"I researched last night for hours after finding out about the murder. This is what I found." Sarah came down the hall, standing in the entryway between the hall and where we stood. A sheet wrapped around her, her hair a mess.

I read the paper Kim had handed me. It took a moment for it to register. I looked at Kim.

"Are you sure?"

Kim nodded. I turned toward Sarah.

"Just how long did Rita Franklin work for your father?"

Sarah stared at both of us and said nothing.

# 45

Sarah looked from one to the other. A confused look on her face.

"I don't know. I didn't know she did."

I handed her the paper. She took it with one hand, the other holding the sheet around her body. Sarah glanced at the paper, then handed it back.

"I didn't know she did," she said.

"Go get dressed, will you?" Kim said.

When Sarah closed the door to the bedroom, Kim looked at me and said,

"Really, Joe. You're not even hiding it."

"I don't think it needs hiding. Besides, she could be in as much danger as anyone."

"I guess she'll be safe in your bed, right?"

"Kim, I know you've never understood my ways. I never asked forgiveness from you for how I behave. I'm not starting now."

"Fine, but when this bites you in the ass like it always does, don't expect me to listen to you cry about it."

She turned away to walk to the window to look out.

"What do we do with this?" I said to her back.

She faced me.

"I sent it to Peter. Maybe you two can come up with something. Don't ask me."

She turned back to the window. I hadn't meant to upset her. But I also didn't want her opinion on something she knew nothing about.

Sarah came from the bedroom, saving me from an embarrassing attempt at Mea culpa. Sarah looked from me to Kim. She came to stand beside me.

"I hope the argument isn't over me," she said, watching Kim.

"It was," Kim said, facing us. "But my opinion isn't wanted, so don't worry about it. I think you're being watched."

I moved to the window to look down onto the street. Kim stood beside me. We both looked down.

"A black car was parked right there."

She pointed to an empty parking place.

"Any ideas?"

"No. Does your girlfriend have an idea?"

I stared at Kim, but the look she gave me kept me from saying anything.

Sarah stood between the two of us. She looked at Kim and said,

"I don't know, but I'm getting scared."

Truth be told, I was getting a little scared myself.

# 46

The night passed with me in a chair, my old .45 in my hand, watching the street. I wouldn't let Kim leave after spotting the car. Kim slept on the couch, Sarah in the bed. Kim thought I was overreacting. Maybe I was. But I would not let anything happen to Kim. Even if I didn't always agree with her, I still cared about her.

Kim sat up on the couch, her hair sticking out on one side of her head. She looked at me through the sleep in her eyes.

"You still mad?"

She nodded her head.

"But I appreciate you worrying."

Sarah came down the hallway from the bedroom. She stood looking at Kim and me, a little unsure what was going on.

"What is the plan today?" she said.

"The plan is, we go downstairs, each go our own way. You two are going to a motel somewhere away from the area. I am going to meet Peter."

I looked at Kim.

"If you even think you spot a tail, you head for the nearest police station or police car you see. Understood?"

Kim nodded. Sarah stared at me wide-eyed.

"I need things from my apartment. I can't just stay in a motel."

Kim stepped forward and took Sarah by the arm, surprising her.

"Listen to him. I don't approve of what you two are doing, but I trust him more than I trust anyone. We do what he says."

Sarah only nodded.

We left the apartment. Kim, with Sarah as a passenger, turned one way. I turned toward the Clover Leaf.

It was a few hours before it opened, but I made a mental appointment to have a drink before the day was over.

I drove to Peter's house. I waited on the porch after I knocked on the door. He came outside in a few minutes, he was dressed in his usual way, sharp.

"We need to go find some connections," I said.

"I know a starting point to connect some."

He pulled his keys from his pocket. I was glad we were taking his car and not my truck. Not that Peter Connolly would ever be caught riding in my truck.

As he started the car, I asked him,

"Where are we going?"

"The castle," he said, referring to the police station.

I experienced a sense of letdown.

"Why there?"

"Webster needs to give us better answers."

## Island Lies

I was silent as we drove to the station. I would be just as happy if I never went back to that place.

# 47

Webster sat behind his desk as the desk sergeant showed us into his office. The sergeant had called ahead. Webster told him to bring us back. Yet he sat like he wasn't expecting us.

"We have questions, Captain," Peter said.

Webster looked at him, surprised to be spoken to so bluntly.

"What questions?"

I closed the door to the office. Webster gave me a look that resembled confusion. Peter sat in a chair in front of the desk.

"I want to know what you found about the fire at my building."

"I found out you're screwed. No insurance, no video. I guess you had a crappy alarm system from the debris we found."

Webster said 'we' as if he had dug through the ashes himself. Every one of us knew he hadn't.

"I had an audible alarm, that was all."

"Not good enough. It looks like it started in the underground garage."

"Any suspects?" he asked.

"One. But he didn't have insurance, so I can't see him burning his building for no gain."

Peter stood and looked down at Webster.

"You think I torched my building?"

"You have a better idea?"

To break up the tension, I said,

"What about Rita Franklin?"

Webster looked over at me. Pete sat in his chair.

".22 caliber. Back of the head, twice. An execution."

"Who owned the house?" I asked.

"I don't know. A corporation I haven't been able to track the owner of." He looked through a file on his desk. "Island Housing, LLC."

"Never heard of them," Pete said.

"The house on Rice is the only thing they own as far as I know."

"Can we get a copy of that?" I asked.

"No. Go to the appraisal office like I did."

"Do you still think these things aren't connected? The firc, my mugging and warning, the murder."

Webster stood, looking at both of us.

"My guess is you two knot heads got yourselves into something that nobody may ever piece together. You both are bottom feeders." He pointed at Peter. "You have so many shady clients, one of them may have burned your place for revenge for shoddy work."

He pointed at me.

"And you, I've known you long enough. I'd like to punch you a few times myself. My only question is, how did they refrain from killing your sorry ass? Now get out of my office."

# 48

In the parking lot, Peter looked back at the double doors of the police station.

"You made him mad."

"I've been kicked out of better places," I said.

We got in the car. Peter started the engine, then looked at me.

"What do you know about arson?"

"It's a felony."

"It is. We are going to look at what's left of my office."

On the drive over, we were silent. When we arrived in front of the rubble, I had no words. I was feeling bad for Pete and what he had lost.

"How's Kim and Sarah?" he asked as we got out of the car.

It occurred to me I did not know what motel they would stay at. I didn't have a cell phone or any way of contacting them.

"Can you call Kim later and see where they are?"

"You need a cell phone, Joe."

We stepped onto the sidewalk and stared at what remained of one of the nicest buildings in this part of town. Which was nothing. There were tape and wooden barricades in place to keep people from getting too close to the scene. We crossed those barriers.

There was a hole that had been an underground parking garage. It was now filled with what was left of the offices that once stood above it.

The city had removed the unstable walls, crashing them into the giant hole as well. The office was nothing but a giant trash pit.

"Damn shame," Pete said, looking down into the hole.

"How does he know?"

"What?" Pete looked over at me.

"How does Webster know it started in the parking garage? You can't even get to the parking garage for all the stuff in there."

"That fireman told us that night."

"He was making a guess. It was too hot to go in there."

Peter scratched his head.

"What are you saying?"

"I don't know. We have been stopped and pushed away from this investigation from the beginning by Webster. What if he knows something we don't?"

"Let's see if we can find who owns Island Housing, LLC."

"Kim's busy."

"I'll call Barbara. Have her get on it. She's working from home now."

He took out his cell phone and made the call. In the meantime, I wanted to find Astrid Franklin and talk to her about her mother.

# 49

Astrid wasn't at the hospital. She was at home. I didn't have her home address. Pete called the hospital, and by impersonating a peace officer, got her home address. We drove over.

It was a nice house in a little neighborhood that was designed for professional working people. Brick houses, paved driveways. Probably not hurricane strong.

It surprised her to see us at her door. She looked at Pete, then at me.

"Yes."

"I'm sorry about your mother," I said.

She nodded, but said nothing.

"Do you have any idea who could have done such a thing to her? Or why?" Pete asked.

Tears rolled down her cheeks.

"No. They say she was murdered. But I don't understand. Who would want to hurt her?"

"Remember the last time we spoke? I told you, I think some things are connected to the past. I believe your mother's murder is one of those things. As well as your sister's death," I said.

She stared straight ahead for a moment, then backed up to allow us in the house. The inside of the house was tastefully decorated. You could tell she lived alone.

"What do you mean?" she asked.

She didn't offer us a drink or a seat. We stood in the middle of the main room.

"Did you know your mom worked for Ben Collier?"

She nodded.

"She did expenses and payroll for him."

"Is that how Emily knew Diana?"

She shrugged. Not answering.

"Who did she buy the house on Rice Street from?" Peter asked.

Astrid turned her back to us and raised her arms in the air.

"Why all these questions? I don't know the answer to any of them."

"Look, I know you were a kid when Diana Collier went missing. A young kid who knew nothing about what was going on. But you know why your mother moved from a nice neighborhood to Welfare City. We need to know," Pete said.

She was crying when she turned back toward us.

"But I don't. Emily died. Mom got sad, and we moved to that place," she said, with contempt in her voice.

"What about her job?" I asked.

"I don't know when she quit working. She never had a decent job after we moved to Rice Street."

"Have you had any strange things happening lately?"

"Other than you two showing up asking questions, you mean?"

I thanked her for her time, and we left the house. On the way to Pete's house and my truck, he tried calling Kim again. No answer. It was still early. Maybe they were settling in.

As Pete and I parted ways, I got in my truck, thinking about a drink. I headed for the Clover Leaf.

# 50

The bar wasn't busy yet, only a few patrons sat at tables scattered around the place. No one was at the bar. Amanda saw me coming and began fixing my drink. She gave me a strange look as she made it.

"What happened to you?"

"As if you don't know?"

"I don't. You look like you got beat up."

I told her about what happened a few nights ago in the alleyway. She set my drink in front of me as she listened.

"I didn't know that. Are you OK?"

I nodded, then said,

"I heard you guys in here knew. Someone told that woman I have been in here with a few times."

"Nobody tells me nothing."

I downed my drink in a single sip. I waited for her to fix me another one. I sipped this one, savoring it.

I wondered which bartender had told Sarah about me getting attacked. Thinking of Sarah, I realized I missed her. That was a strange feeling for me. Missing someone.

But I did. She filled a vacuum in me somewhere I couldn't describe. I finished my drink. I waved at Amanda as I stood from my stool.

"Leaving already?"

"I'll see you soon."

I walked to my apartment. The sun was on its way down, it would be dark soon. The heat of the day was fading as night approached.

I fixed a drink, then sat on my couch. I picked up the phone and dialed Kim's number. No answer. I left a message. I tried Sarah's. Same results.

I was beginning to worry. One of them should have called by now to let me know where they were and if they were safe. There was a killer on the loose after all.

I was getting ready for a shower when the phone rang. I grabbed it expecting one of the women's voices. Instead, it was Webster.

"You need to come to the E.R. now," he said, he sounded agitated.

"Why?"

"I'll explain when I see you."

He hung up. I got dressed and headed to the hospital.

Webster was standing with Pete Connolly as I walked in through the E.R. doors. My pulse quickened as I thought of Sarah and Kim.

Pete looked at me as I walked up.

"This is bad, Joe."

"Is it Kim? Or Sarah?"

Webster shook his head.

"Rita Franklin's daughter. Astrid. She was attacked in her home earlier. Neighbors walking their dog called 911 when they heard her screams." I looked at each man. I couldn't believe what I was being told.

"Neighbors describe Pete's car and two men matching you fools as being at her house earlier."

"Are we suspects?" Pete asked, leaning against the wall.

"Don't be a jackass." Webster looked at me. "Maybe things are a little more connected than I first thought."

"Thanks for noticing. Observations like that, you'll make detective someday," I said.

Webster ignored me. He said,

"She looks like hell. Someone worked her over pretty good. She'll be OK, though."

"Can we see her?"

He shook his head.

"They gave her pain meds. I got her statement and Officer Jameson is taking pictures of the injuries. I suggest we go to the station and talk."

For the first time I could remember, I agreed with Captain Webster.

# 51

As we sat around Webster's desk, I mentioned to Pete I hadn't heard from Kim or Sarah since this morning when we left my apartment. He said he hadn't either.

Fishing in his desk drawer, Webster set a small voice recorder on his desk. He pushed the red record button and spoke into it, telling who was in the room and the time.

I told Webster all we knew, ending with the events of the day and our visit to Astrid Franklin's house.

He picked up the recorder, holding it close to his face.

"For the record, these two men are not suspects."

He hit the stop button and set the recorder aside.

"Where do you think Kim and Sarah are?"

I shrugged.

"I don't know, but I'm starting to worry."

"OK. We have a guy out there committing assaults and murders to hide his involvement with the original crime of kidnapping twenty-two years ago."

Pete nodded.

"As crazy as it sounds, yeah."

"The murders aren't new," I said.

"How so?" Webster said.

"They started about ten years ago. Bob Reeves and Emily Franklin."

"No dice on either one. Reeves was in a car crash on Island Drive. I don't know about this Emily girl."

"Island Drive? Why was he over there?" I asked.

Webster shrugged his shoulder.

"He was investigating the Collier case. It was cold by then, but he had just been assigned the case a few weeks before. He was chasing leads."

"His widow told me the crash happened coming back from the parents' house."

Webster sat up in his chair.

"She did?"

I nodded.

Pete's phone rang. I looked at him as he answered. He said 'hello' twice, then handed me the phone.

I took it, held the phone to my ear. After my hello I heard Kim's voice saying my name. Over and over.

She sounded far away, like the phone was on one side of the room and she was on the other, trying to talk.

"Joe? Can you hear me?"

It kept repeating rapidly, giving me no time to answer. I pushed the speaker button on the phone. The repeated questions filled the room. We all listened.

The line went dead. My heart rate quickened. I tried calling the number back. It was Kim's cell number. It went straight to voicemail.

I stood, looking at both men. All I was thinking was, what in the hell was going on?

# 52

"Give me her phone number."

I wrote it down on a sticky note. Webster stood, taking the note.

"We can ping it on reverse 911. It's not always accurate but sometimes it is."

He left Pete and me alone in his office. I sat down in the chair I had jumped up from earlier.

"That didn't sound good at all."

Pete nodded as he scrolled through his phone.

"I need to call Barbara and check on her."

Pete pushed his screen several times, then held the phone to his ear. He stepped out of the office into the hall.

I sat alone. Worried.

Pete came back into the office. He sat down. He called Kim's phone again as he said,

"Barbara is OK. She's home and nobody's getting past those Dobermans she has."

He pushed the end button on the phone, shaking his head.

Webster came back into the room. He stood by the door as he said,

"The ping came back to an address for a hotel on Fox. I have a unit on the way, we can meet them. Let's go."

We were out the door in a hurry. I rode with Pete as he followed Webster's unit to the motel on Fox Street.

Why Kim chose this area for a motel I could only guess. It was not in a good location as Fox Street was the heart of the drug center. Dealers, prostitutes, and other criminal activities were the main income source in this part of the city.

We all pulled into the parking lot of the Sand Land motel. A single level motel that offered hourly as well as daily rates.

The parking lot was empty except for a patrol cruiser sitting in front of an open door, its lights off. I was going to be sick, thinking what that could mean.

I got out of the car and ran to the open door. Officer Jameson, standing inside the doorway, tried to keep me out of the room. I pushed past him. Webster and Pete behind me. Jameson relaxed.

Kim was sitting in the chair at the small table by the window. She had a bruise on her head above her right eye, and her wrists were chaffed where they had been tied to the chair, showing a little blood.

There was no sign of Sarah. I kneeled in front of Kim, taking her hand in mine.

"Are you OK?"

She shook her head.

"I'm a damn fool."

Tears fell on her lap. I wanted to wipe them away. Anger boiling in me at whoever had done this to her.

"What happened? Where's Sarah?"

"She got a call. Said she'd be back. About a half hour later, there was a knock on the door. I thought it was her. A man...hit me as I opened the door. I woke up tied to this chair. My phone was over by the bathroom. I had to try several times to get it to voice dial."

"An ambulance is on its way," Jameson said behind me.

I helped Kim stand up. I hugged her as she wrapped her arms around me.

"Where the hell is Sarah?" I asked.

No one answered.

# 53

We stood in the parking lot watching the ambulance pull out. I had convinced Kim to go get checked out. I held her keys in her hand.

"How did Sarah go wherever she went without a car?" I said, looking at Kim's keys.

"I'm more interested in where she went," Pete said.

A taxi pulled into the parking lot. Not a yellow cab like on TV, the island had nothing like that. This was a maroon minivan, with the words Island Taxi on the doors.

The sliding door opened, and Sarah stepped out of the van. She came running toward us. I hugged her in front of everyone, not caring what they thought. I held her tight as I said,

"Where have you been?"

"I had to go see my parents. I told Kim I'd be back. What happened?" she said, breaking the embrace.

Before I could tell her anything, Webster interrupted.

"Before all that, ma'am. I'd like to ask you a few questions. Alone," he said, showing his gold badge.

Sarah looked at me for a moment as Webster took her by the arm and guided her to a spot beside Jameson's patrol unit.

I stood next to Peter watching them. I could feel Peter looking at me.

"What?" I said, not taking my eyes off Sarah.

"Odd isn't it. She not being here when Kim was attacked. Showing up after."

I looked at him. He was staring at me.

"What do you know about her?"

"I know enough that I'm not answering your questions about it. She is as much a victim as anyone else in this."

Peter nodded.

"You're right. Sorry. What do we do about whoever attacked Kim?"

"Unless there is a marauding gang of attackers on the loose, it's probably the same one who attacked Astrid."

"I know a place to start."

I turned to face him.

"Where?"

"Her parents," he said, motioning his head toward Sarah.

It wasn't a bad idea. It would be a chance to talk to her folks again. This time I had more knowledge than I did before.

I reminded myself knowledge doesn't equal intelligence.

# 54

I took Kim's car to my place. Sarah rode with me. Pete and I agreed to meet in the morning and go talk to the Colliers. I decided not to let Sarah know. She had been upset with me the last time I spoke with her parents. I didn't need that now.

In my apartment, in the bedroom, we undressed. I held her naked body next to me, feeling her shiver. I stroked her hair.

"I'm sorry about Kim. I shouldn't have left her."

"What did your folks need that was so important?"

"My mom. Dad wasn't home. Mom hates being alone since Diana... She called me to come sit with her."

I had no words. You couldn't be angry at someone for being there for a parent. I held her tighter.

We slept through the night, holding each other as we lay there. She flinched occasionally as she slept, from what I didn't know. I hugged her tighter every time she did.

The morning came too fast for me. I enjoyed being in her arms, feeling her body heat next to me under the blanket.

We dressed without talking much. Something seemed between us, I couldn't tell what. "Will you check on Kim today?" she asked, pulling her shirt on.

I nodded. Still not wanting to tell her about talking to her parents.

"I need to go home, get some clothes, clean up a little."

"OK. I don't want you gone too much. Come back here as soon as you can."

I kissed her a soft kiss as I got ready to leave. Pete was to meet me downstairs to go to the Colliers' together.

As we drove to the Collier house, I was still feeling at odds. Kim had refused to stay in the hospital. She was at home resting. I should check on her. Instead, I was going with Pete on a wild goose chase.

The Collier house was as I remembered. Nothing seemed out of place as we knocked on the door.

Marie Collier answered the door. She looked as if she had eaten something sour when she saw us.

"Mrs. Collier is your husband home. We have questions," Pete said.

She nodded and invited us in. She said nothing as she led us to a den, where Ben Collier was watching CNN.

He muted the TV as we entered. He looked at us and placed the remote on the table beside the chair.

"Mr. Connolly, and I don't remember your name, but I remember your raggedy truck."

"Langley," I said.

"We have questions for you, if you don't mind," Pete said.

"I do mind," he said, standing to face us.

157

He looked at me and I said,

"Well, in that case, how long did Rita Franklin work for you?"

"Rita Franklin? I heard she was killed. Why do you want to know?"

Pete looked at me.

"All that talking, but no answers," he said.

Collier stared at us as if we were the ones daft.

"She worked for my company for about six years. She did financials for me."

"When did she leave the company?" Pete said.

Collier was thinking, or stalling.

"Was Sarah here last night?" I asked.

The question caught him off guard.

"Where my daughter goes is little concern for either of you."

"Actually, it is," Pete said.

"Someone assaulted my secretary not long after Sarah left her alone."

"Tragic," he said, walking toward the doorway we had just entered. "You both can go now."

Collier didn't lead us out. He simply pointed toward the front door. Marie led us to the entrance or exit in this case.

Before she shut the door on us, I turned to her and said,

"Was Sarah here last night?"

The only answer I got was the door closing.

# 55

We drove around the block looking at the area Diana Collier had called home and had felt safe in. It looked different back then. The basketball court was a nice park now.

"What an ass," Pete said as he drove.

"Stop the car."

He pulled off the main lane and came to a stop. I got out before the car completely stopped. Pete fell in behind me as I led the way to the fountain.

A small fountain, a small vertical spray of water in the center. What had caught my eye was the plaque, mounted on a rock base beside the fountain. Pete stopped beside me as we read the engraving on it. The writing weathered and hard to read in places.

*We hereby dedicate this park and fountain to the citizens of the neighborhood of Big Beach to be enjoyed by current, former, and future residents. This ground will forever be known as Diana's Garden.*

The date of dedication was only a few months after Diana disappeared. The writing at the bottom was hard to read. Pete knelt and read aloud. *Made possible by the partnership of Benjamin Collier and Micheal Holt.*

Pete straightened and looked at me. I was staring at the plaque as if it held answers.

"Is Micheal Holt, Mickey?" Pete asked.

I only nodded. I looked around the park, trying to picture it how it was before. Before the fountain, the flowers, before the shrubs that circled the walking path that went around the park. The basketball court where a young girl enjoyed spending her free time. Hoping to make the high school team.

As Pete turned away, I grabbed his arm, stopping him.

"I want to know what else they partnered on."

"I hear you, pal. I want to know how I and everyone else missed this big ass clue in the middle of a park."

# 56

Pete dropped me at the hospital, where my truck was. I needed to talk to Astrid Franklin about her attack. It seemed like weeks ago, but it was only a night ago.

I rode the elevator to the floor with patient rooms and found the room number they gave me at the front desk.

I knocked before entering. Astrid lay on the bed, a big bandage covering the left side of her face. Shielding one eye. She had IVs in her left arm. The machine at her head showed the status of her vitals.

I stood beside her bed.

"Astrid, I'm Joe Langley. You remember me?"

She nodded.

"Do you know who did this to you?"

She shook her head. Her voice was weak when she said,

"I don't know. A man. Dressed in black. He just kept punching me."

Tears fell from her one eye.

"A friend of mine was attacked last night, too. A man in black. At a hotel on Fox."

161

"I'm sorry for your friend."

She didn't look at me. She stared down at her blanket instead.

"Did the man say anything to you?"

She shook her head.

"He was in my house..."

Tears fell faster as she shook from the effort of crying.

I took hold of her hand.

"You're alive. There's that. Your mom isn't."

She looked up at me.

"You think this is about that old case?"

"I do. I need answers to a lot of questions. But it's connected."

She wiped her eye with the blanket. She took a deep breath and said,

"You can search my mom's place if you think it will help."

The adrenaline pumped through my veins, causing me to stand straighter. A search of the house was what I was hoping for.

The police would have searched already. But I was looking for different things than they were.

I said goodbye to her and promised to keep her informed. I drove to the house on Rice Street as fast as island traffic allowed.

I had a ton of questions. I needed answers. I pulled up to the house and looked around outside before coming back to the porch.

## Island Lies

I hadn't been to a murder scene in ages. I hoped I knew what I was doing.

# 57

I stepped onto the old porch and tried the doorknob. It was unlocked. I broke the yellow crime scene tape that covered the doorway and went inside.

The iron smell of blood was strong in the small house. The hallway, which was nothing more than a small narrow corridor, had a dark splotch of dried blood in the center of the floor. Looking around the house, nothing looked disturbed. There were no signs of forced entry. Did Rita know her killer? Or, like her daughter, found him already in the house.

There were two bedrooms and a bathroom down the short hall. The center bedroom must have been Astrids when she was a teenager. It was a junk room now. Old clothes, broken furniture, and small appliances were stacked everywhere. What caught my eye was the file cabinet against the far wall.

Stepping over piles of clothes, black trash bags, and junk, I tripped, falling against the file cabinet. The jar made my ribs flame in pain.

I took a moment to gather myself, then pulled on the top drawer handle. It opened easily. The drawer was empty. The next two were too. The last drawer had a single file folder in it.

Lying flat on the bottom of the drawer was a blue folder. I picked it up. Inside were two pieces of paper stapled together.

I read over it. A contract for the house I was now standing in. On the second page was a place for signatures.

Rita Franklin's was on the left side of the page, the buyer side. The right side, the seller side, had one signature. Island Housing, LLC. An initial next to the name of the company. MH.

I folded the contract and stuck it in my pocket. I backtracked through the room, stepping into the small hallway.

James Webster was standing at the front door, his pistol in his hand. He looked at me as he holstered the gun.

"What are you doing in my crime scene?"

"The daughter said I could look around."

"We searched the scene already. You're standing where she died," he pointed to the dark stain I stood in.

I took a step forward.

"Any ideas on who did it?"

Webster stepped out on the porch, forcing me to follow him. Once outside, he reattached the crime scene tape. As he worked, he said,

"No. But we are assuming it was someone she knew. We are looking into her social life, and her friends here in the area. The usual."

The contract I had folded in my pocket felt conspicuous, like Webster would know I had it. He turned toward me after he finished fixing the tape.

"What did you find?"

"Just an empty file cabinet. And a very messy house," I lied and didn't feel bad about it.

"Well, one thing for sure. If she had lived, Rita Franklin could have caught a charge for felony housekeeping."

He stepped off the porch and walked back to his car. I went to my truck. We both left going separate ways. Webster back to the station, I assumed. I headed home.

# 58

Sarah was at my place when I got home. She wore cotton shorts that showed a lot of legs and a baggy Astros T-shirt.

She kissed me as soon as I laid my keys down on the counter. I kissed her back, fighting the urge to take her there in the living room.

I broke the embrace and stared into her eyes. She was smiling. She was becoming a weakness in me. I could feel it.

She made me feel things that were long silent inside me. I loved being around her, but this case was the only reason we had met. She wanted to find out what happened to her sister.

Now, there were dozens of other questions. I had placed the contract I had taken from the Franklin house in my glove box. I didn't want it just lying around.

She kissed me again as we stood looking at each other. I didn't fight the urge this time.

After we got dressed, we went to the bar. We both needed drinks. Though I knew she had been drinking already, a little anyway.

Sitting at the bar, Amanda fixed me my usual and took Sarah's order. She brought both drinks in no time.

I took a long drink, then looked at Sarah and said,

"I went to see Astrid Franklin again."

Sarah held up a hand, stopping me from saying more.

"I don't want to talk about the case tonight. Please. Too much has happened, too many people have been hurt and it's my fault."

I sipped my drink.

"How is it your fault?"

"I keep digging into the case when everyone tells me to stop. I dug so much that people have died."

I stared at the bar top in front of me and thought of what she said. I ordered another drink.

"Things are in motion now, for sure. Even if you wanted to, you can't stop what is happening."

"I don't want to stop it. I just need to think about it."

That statement confused me, but I said nothing. Amanda brought the cordless phone to me, holding it out toward me.

"It's for you," she said, placing it on the bar top.

I took it and placed it to my ear and said hello.

I disconnected the call, then looked at Sarah.

"I have to go. You can stay at my place if you need to."

She looked at me as I got up to leave.

"Where are you going?"

"That was Kim. She needs me over at her place now."

"Leaving me for another woman? I should be jealous," she said, standing to kiss me.

I kissed her back. I left without a word.

# 59

I drove to Kim's house. Pete Connolly's car was already there, along with a car I didn't recognize. I wondered what she wanted. All she said on the phone was to get over to her place now.

I knocked on the door. Pete let me in. He led me to the kitchen where Kim and Pete's secretary, Barbara, were sitting in the dining chairs around the table. Papers covered the surface of the table. Both women looked up as Pete and I walked in.

"Joe, look at this," Kim said, holding a paper out to me.

I took it. It was a printout from the tax assessor's website for the county. It had a parcel ID number, which meant nothing to me. It also had an address on it. The address was for the little park in the Big Beach, the one now known as Diana's Garden.

I must have taken too long to see what she wanted me to see, because Kim said,

"The name of the owners."

I glanced at the bottom of the page. It didn't belong to the city as I had thought when looking at it. It was privately owned. By Island Housing LLC.

"This makes sense," I said.

Pete looked at me and said,

"You don't seem surprised. We all were. I thought the city owned that park, as well maintained as it is."

I didn't say anything. I went to my truck to get the paperwork I had taken earlier. I brought it in and handed it to Pete. He read it, then passed it to the women.

"The same company that owns the park owned Franklin's house," Barbara said.

"The initial beside the signature. MH. Mickey Holt," I said.

Pete took the paper from Kim. He looked at it again.

"Mickey Holt," Pete said.

I nodded.

"My landlord. He sold you your building a few weeks ago. He sold the dead lady a house, and he owns the park dedicated to the missing girl we have all been looking for."

"I don't believe in coincidences," Kim said. "His name is all over this mess. We need to talk to him," I said.

Pete agreed. We left Kim and Barbara at the table to continue their research. Pete and I, in my truck this time, went to visit Mickey Holt at his office downtown.

We were silent on the drive. I didn't know what Pete was thinking, but I was thinking there may finally be an answer for Sarah after all.

# 60

Mickey Holt's office was in the downtown area around the banking center. A building on Center Street, twenty-seven floors. His office was on the top floor, a corner office.

There was no secretary at the desk when we entered the office. The door to Holt's office was open, so we walked into his office.

He was eating a tuna sandwich, the bag on the desk from a shop around the corner. He looked up at us in surprise.

"Where is Nelda?" he asked, his mouth full of food.

"I don't know Nelda," Pete said.

"We have questions," I said, sitting in a chair in front of his desk.

Pete sat in the one beside me. We stared at Mickey Holt.

"Are you here to pay rent, Joe?"

I shook my head.

"We want to know about Diana's Garden," I said.

"Diana's Garden?" he repeated. "I don't know anything about that. The Colliers take care of that."

"The park sits where the basketball courts were. Whose idea was that park?" Pete asked.

Mickey sat back in his chair. His polo shirt had a food stain in the middle of it. It looked like an old stain.

"The neighborhood, of course."

"Your name is all over Diana Collier's disappearance. You need to explain some things," I said.

Mickey Holt sat up in his chair and leaned his arms on his desk.

"What are you two idiots talking about?"

"A break-in, a fire, and a murder," Pete said. "I did none of those things. You can show yourselves out of my office."

"It's not that easy, Mick. Your name is everywhere we look. Pete's building, which is burned down, my office, which was burglarized and only items involving this case were taken. The murder of a woman who used to work for the father of the missing girl," I said.

"You see how us idiots could believe you are a murdering scumbag?" Pete said.

Mickey Holt stood from behind his desk. He walked over to the door of his office and said,

"Leave now. I will not be accused of something just because I'm wealthy."

I followed Pete from the office. As we rode the elevator down, he said,

"Maybe we pushed too hard."

"I haven't pushed yet. This case has so many lies surrounding it, we need to sort fact from fiction."

The elevator doors opened, and we walked out of the building in silence.

# 61

I met Sarah at the Clover Leaf. She had been there since I had left her earlier. Amanda pointed me toward her.

"Good luck," she said. "I cut her off an hour ago."

She was drunk. Sitting at a table in the corner of the room. In the darkest part of the bar. I stood watching her for a moment. She didn't know I was there.

She drank a glass of clear liquid. I was guessing water, since Amanda had quit serving her booze. Why did Sarah get hammered every night?

I could ask the same question about myself. I knew my reasons though, or thought I did. I wasn't a psychiatrist. I had no business wondering about the psyche of someone else. I walked over to the table. She looked up at me and smiled a drunken smile.

"Hey, handsome. Where have you been?"

"Working. Let's go home."

I took her by the hand and led her outside. I drove to my place. Once inside, we sat on the couch. I didn't think she needed a drink, but I did. I made myself a scotch and her a glass of water. When I handed her the water, she was crying.

"What's wrong?"

"Me. And my thinking."

I didn't know what that meant. She set the water glass on the side table. Kicking off her shoes, she stretched out on the couch, placing her legs in my lap. Soon she was asleep.

I sat there for a little while, sipping my drink and watching her. I had no siblings, certainly, I had never lost anyone like she had lost her sister. I couldn't imagine the emotional toil such a thing took on a person.

I left her on the couch as I went to the bedroom and went to bed.

The next morning when I got up, Sarah was still asleep on the couch. She looked less troubled when she slept like there were no worries in her world.

It was when she was awake, the monsters bothered her. I was feeling bothered today myself.

The meeting with Mickey Holt hadn't gone like I had hoped it would. Pete was sure Mickey was involved. I was too. But I needed proof. I would spend the day surveilling Mickey Holt.

Peter had agreed yesterday to observe the Colliers. We were looking for any connection between the two.

I left my apartment being as quiet as I could, trying to let Sarah sleep as long as she could.

I picked up Mickey Holt's trail as he left his house on Colfax and headed toward his office. I kept my distance. This promised to be a long, boring day.

# 62

For most of the day, I altered my position from sitting in my truck to sitting in a small coffee shop across from Holt's building. The sun reflecting off the buildings and concrete made for a hot day. I wanted to ditch the work and go for a drink. But I stayed.

Mickey Holt came out of his building around two in the afternoon. He got in his car, a Nissan, old and dirty. I followed him at a distance, the traffic was heavy on the main thoroughfare. We crossed over into Welfare City.

The traffic thinned out. I dropped farther back. I knew where he was going. I stopped a block away from Rita Franklin's house.

Mickey Holt's car was parked in front. He tore the tape down and entered the house as I put my truck in park.

He was in there for six minutes according to the clock on the dash. He came out empty-handed, hurrying to his car. He drove away. I waited.

What was he looking for in a dead woman's house? Did he find it? I didn't think so, but I couldn't be sure.

## Island Lies

I drove to my office. Whether it was being repaired or not, it was still my space. The doors to the stairs were fixed. My key still worked. The door entering my office wasn't fixed yet.

I sat at my desk and called Pete Connolly. We agreed to meet at the Clover Leaf later. I walked to my apartment, hoping Sarah was still there.

She was gone, the place empty. Her perfume hung in the air, along with the smell of stale booze. I poured a drink into the glass I used last night. And sat at the counter sipping it, thinking.

I finished my drink and went to the bar. I was hoping Pete had something more than I did.

We sat at a table in the center of the bar. I had my scotch. Pete drank coffee. I told him about Mickey Holt and listened as he told me about his day. There were few people in the bar, it was still early in the day. After he finished talking, I said,

"That's it. Nothing happened, nobody went anywhere?"

"Ben nor Marie left the house. Only Sarah visited for a few minutes with her dad in the driveway."

"I thought my day sucked."

"What do you think Holt was looking for?"

"I don't know," I said, shaking my head. "I don't even know if he found anything."

"The police didn't find the paperwork. You did. Maybe that was all that was valuable in there."

"I'm going home and having a stiff drink or two."

I left Pete sitting at the table with his coffee. I needed something much stronger.

# 63

Sarah was at my place. When I walked in, she greeted me at the door with a kiss. I was thinking a man could get used to that. She broke the embrace and picked up her glass from the side table. She handed it to me, and I took a long sip.

"You want some?" she asked.

Assuming she was talking about the scotch, I nodded my head.

She hugged me again.

"Were you busy today?" I asked.

She stepped back and shook her head. She went to the kitchen and was making our drinks when she said,

"No. Went home to clean up a bit, change clothes. I have been here most of the day. How was your day?"

I hesitated, just a beat.

"Boring. No new developments."

"That's not good. I was hoping to have this done by now."

She handed me my glass. I looked into her eyes. She had lied to me. Why?

That was a question I would explore later. Now, I drank my scotch and watched a beautiful woman smile at me in a way that raised my blood.

We finished our drinks and then went to the bedroom. After we were finished, we lay there holding each other. I was getting used to this. It scared me.

I didn't know a lot about her. I knew she drank so we had that in common. I didn't know if we had anything else in common beyond the physical.

I looked forward to exploring all these things with her. But she was right. We should have had some answers to this case by now. Instead, we only had a ton of questions.

Sarah breathed deeply as she lay next to me. I stroked her hair. A man could get used to this.

# 64

The next morning, I slept in. Sarah was up rummaging around in the kitchen. I could smell coffee brewing and food cooking.

I stumbled to the kitchen in my underwear. She glanced at me and smiled. She was drinking coffee. I didn't know if it was spiked with anything stronger than creamer or not.

"Morning. Are you hungry?"

"Yeah, I'm starving."

She fixed an omelet and plated it for me. She fixed one for herself as well. I wolfed it down. It felt as if I'd not eaten in days. We ate in silence. I was still thinking of the lie she had told me last night.

The phone rang. I got up and answered it, taking the call in the living room instead of walking back to the kitchen counter.

I listened to Kim say she needed to see me and Pete at once. I hung up the phone.

"I have to go."

I went to the bedroom and got dressed. Sarah was standing in the hallway watching me.

"Something important?"

"I don't know yet. Maybe."

Kim had said she had called Pete already. I drove to her house, anticipating what she and Barbara had found.

When Kim let me into her house, we were the only ones there. She led me to the kitchen table that they had sat around the day before.

"Joe, you know I care for you. Even if I don't agree with how you live your life, I have always had your back. Right?"

"True. You've been a solid friend to me. Why are you talking like this?"

"Sit down," she said, pointing to a chair.

I took a seat, and she held up a paper and said,

"In digging through the finances of the Collier's, Barbara found this."

She handed me the paper. I read it once, then again.

"How'd you get this?"

"Barbara can hack into anything. She makes me look like you when it comes to computers."

"How long?"

"Twenty years it looks like. Same doctor. He is either not very good or Sarah is a screwed-up woman."

I read the printout again. It was a bank statement from an account in Benjamin Collier's name. The only expense from the account was to Dr. Felix Amber. The total looked to be hundreds of thousands of dollars.

Dr. Amber was a psychiatrist. And a very poor one it seemed, he had treated Sarah for two decades, until a few months ago.

I didn't wait for Pete. I wanted to talk to Dr. Amber, now.

# 65

Felix Amber's office was in the medical district of the city. A multi-story hospital took up most of a city block, while across the street and along another stretch of city block were the clinic and office buildings. Amber's office was on the seventh floor, in the middle of the hallway. I entered an outer office that seemed no bigger than a broom closet. A secretary sat behind a cramped half divider in the wall. She looked at me and tried to smile.

"I need to see Dr. Amber please."

"Do you have an appointment?"

I looked around the tiny waiting room. Four people sat in chairs that were too close together, staring at me.

I pointed at a door, and asked the lady behind the desk,

"Is he in there?"

I walked to the door and knocked hard. The secretary came from behind her cubby hole trying to get me to stop, repeating herself. I kept knocking harder each time.

The door opened in a rush. A man in shirt sleeves, tie loose at the neck, said,

"What is the meaning of this?"

I looked past him for a moment, surprised to see the soles of two shoes poking up from a long couch. People really laid down to talk to these guys?

The man was balding, his beard trimmed neatly.

"I need to talk to you, now."

"I can see you are in distress sir, but you will have to wait your turn."

I was tired of playing games. I wanted to punch him. Instead, I said,

"It will only take a minute. It's about a patient."

"Sir, I will not give out confidential information on a patient."

"What if I break your nose, will you then?"

"Sir, violence is never an..."

I grabbed him by the shirt front and pushed him into his office. The patient on the couch sat up watching us.

"Sarah Collier," I said, pulling my hand back to punch him.

"I can't discuss that."

He closed his eyes, waiting for a hit. I released him instead.

"Thanks Doc, you gave me what I was looking for."

I left Amber's office feeling disgusted with myself. It had been a long time since I had resorted to threatening anyone for information. But this case had me reeling.

Not knowing what else to do, I drove back to Kim's house.

# 66

Pete was at Kim's house when I got there. He was sitting at the table drinking coffee with Kim and Barbara. Pete looked at me as I walked in and said,

"Any luck?"

"Enough to know he knows who she is."

"He told you that?" Barbara asked.

"I threatened to punch him," I said.

"Oh Lord, Joe," Kim said, shaking her head.

Pete sipped his coffee, then said,

"It means nothing in the long run. People see shrinks for a lot of reasons. And the woman had a pretty traumatic childhood. I'd be worried if she hadn't been talking to someone."

"How many shrinks would condone the drinking? I assume she wasn't a drunk at sixteen, so that means it's an occurrence since she was seeing Amber," I said.

"Then why would her father spend the money from a separate account to have her in therapy?" Barbara asked.

No one had an answer. Into the silence I said,

"She lied to me last night. Maybe unintentional, but she did lie."

"About what?" Pete said.

"Visiting her father."

"Maybe she didn't think it was important to mention. It was a brief meeting," Pete said.

I nodded. Possibly, I thought. I felt guilty questioning Sarah's actions behind her back. Like I was cheating on her.

She didn't deserve it. She was the one who had spent her money and time looking into her sister's disappearance. She thought a stranger had done it. It looked more likely that a friend of the family was involved. More precisely, Mickey Holt was suspect number one.

"OK, how much more do we know about Mickey Holt's involvement in this mess?" I said.

Kim shook her head. Barbara gave a frown, and Pete said nothing.

"That's our priority. I'll go talk to Mickey again."

"Alone?" Pete asked.

"Yeah, it may be more effective without you. He don't like you."

"You think you're on his Christmas card list?"

"Maybe not. Kim, can you two keep digging into Island Housing? I feel that's the key to this. Pete, you can talk to Webster. I want to know what exactly they found in Franklin's house."

I left them sitting at the table, staring at me. It had been a long time since I felt like I was in command. But I was feeling it now. It felt good. I might celebrate later with a drink.

# 67

I drove to Mickey Holt's office, hoping he'd be there. I was questioning myself on how to confront him. I didn't know what Holt's values were. Honesty, character. Who knew?

I rode the elevator to the floor and went into his office door. An older woman sat behind the outer office desk this time. When she saw me, her facial expression changed to resemble someone who had just eaten a mouthful of lemons.

I didn't stop at her desk. I passed her by going to Holt's office. She didn't stop me. Mickey Holt sat with his legs up on his desk, and his hands behind his head. He turned to look at me and groaned aloud as I walked in and sat in the chair I had sat in earlier.

"Damn, Langley. Don't you ever wait to be announced. I pay Nelda a good salary to announce people."

"You might not see me if I did that."

"Possible. After last time."

"You're not going to enjoy this time, either."

He placed his feet on the floor, and his arms on the chair arms. He made a sound in his throat.

"Are you here to accuse me of something again?"

"I'm here to ask questions, hoping you won't lie to me."

"Then, for God's sake, ask and then leave."

"Island Housing. How long have you owned the company?"

"It's a dead company. There are a few holdings in it. Low return stuff I don't waste time with."

"It has a few curious holdings, though. Rita Franklin's house, the area known as Diana's Garden. Connolly's building. Weird thing is, I connected all those places to the missing girl we are looking for."

Mickey Holt leaned back in his chair, smiling at me.

"Here comes the allegations."

"What were you looking for at Franklin's house?"

His smile disappeared. He looked down at his desk, then back at me.

"You followed me? Why?"

"Because I think you had something to do with either the girl's disappearance years ago, or Rita Frankin's murder, or both."

He stood and walked to his window. He looked down at Center Street. He shook his head in frustration. Without turning, he said,

"I had nothing to do with any of those things. I surely never killed anyone. I am not responsible for that girl's disappearance."

"Why search the house?"

"Island Housing is an embarrassment for me. I didn't want anyone to find any document that would lead to me. Luckily, there was none that I found."

"That's because I found it."

He turned to face me. I thought I saw panic in his eyes. Only a moment, then it was gone. Anger was all I could see.

"The police have it now. Maybe you'll answer their questions since you avoided most of mine."

I stood and walked toward the door. Before I left, he said,

"Joe. Perhaps when this is over, you need to find another office. We seem to be unable to work together."

I kept walking.

# 68

I didn't go back to Kim's house. Someone needed to tail Mickey Holt. I volunteered for the job. I wanted to see if I had shaken him up any. If so, where did he go? Who would he meet with?

Fifteen minutes after I left his office, so did he. I tailed him in my old truck from a farther distance than before. He would most likely be looking for a tail now that he knew he had been followed once.

He drove in a direct path for the most part. Until he left the business district and headed into the residential and commercial areas.

He would make a sudden turn onto a side street. I would follow him on a bordering street and catch up to him at one of the lights.

I kept that game up until I realized where he was trying to ultimately go. I backed off farther, allowing him to feel safe.

I parked a few vehicles down the street as he pulled into a spot to parallel park in front of a building. My heart hammered in my chest as I watched Sarah Collier come from inside her apartment building to get into his car.

They pulled away. I followed. From a distance, I couldn't see what was happening in the car. Was Sarah in danger?

She had got into the car voluntarily, without him getting out to get her. She was with him because she had wanted to go.

She was at my apartment when I left earlier. When did she come to her place? Why?

I slapped the steering wheel in frustration. There were too damn many questions, and I still wasn't close to any answers.

Mickey Holt must not have been worried about being followed since he picked up Sarah. He drove in a mostly straight route to the next stop. Big Beach. Sarah's parents' house.

I stopped two blocks down the street and watched as Sarah and Holt got out of the car and went to the door of the house.

Ben Collier opened the door and allowed them inside. I noted the time on my truck's clock. Two hours later, it was dark. They came out and Ben stood on the porch as Mickey Holt and Sarah backed out of the driveway.

I wondered if Sarah would come to my place tonight. I followed Holt's car again, holding back a ways to avoid being too suspicious if he was watching. He drove Sarah back to her apartment and dropped her off. He left. I didn't follow.

Waiting four minutes by the clock, I went up to Sarah's apartment and knocked on the door. She still wore the clothes she had on earlier. She looked surprised to see me. She recovered fast, though.

"Joe, I was going to call you and tell you I wouldn't be there tonight."

"I thought you'd be here when you weren't at my place."

She invited me in. I followed her to the now familiar old couch.

"I have been neglecting this place too much. I need to clean some things up."

"I don't need to stay. I just wanted to know you were OK."

She kissed me. A quick kiss on the lips.

"Can I tell you something?" she said, stepping back.

I nodded.

"Sure."

"I think I'm falling in love with you. Is that OK?"

I was speechless. Everything I wanted to say fell away. I kissed her, hard and passionately. It conflicted me to hear her say those words. If I had not known where she had been just a few hours earlier, I'd have been happy. Now, I was confused.

Even in my confusion, I drank her booze and stayed the night.

# 69

Sarah was sleeping the next morning as I left her apartment. I had a sleepless night after we had done our thing. She had repeated the words I love you several times. I couldn't say anything back to her. It was awkward, both hearing those words and my silence.

I couldn't say what Sarah wanted to hear. First, I wasn't sure I felt the same at all. She was a good woman to hang out with, share a drink, have some laughs, among other things. But I wasn't the fall in love type of guy. I enjoyed my freedom too much.

The second reason, I didn't know if I could trust her. Her being with Mickey Holt after I had visited him confused me.

I needed more answers than I had. I drove to Pete's house, hoping he would be awake at this early hour. I had no idea what he was going to do about finding an office. For that matter, I didn't either. Mickey Holt had practically kicked me out of mine.

Pete answered his door, coffee cup in hand, looking sharp and flawless. His suit must have cost more than my rent. I felt a pang of jealousy for a moment.

"We need to talk," I said.

He stepped aside and let me in. He led me to the kitchen and offered me a cup of coffee. I accepted.

"I talked to Mickey Holt yesterday."

"Get anywhere?" he asked, as he handed me my coffee cup.

"I think I got evicted. But more than that, after I left his office, I tailed him. He picked up Sarah and went to her parents' house."

Pete looked at me. His face contorted into a look of pain as he thought about what I said.

"What the hell is that about?"

I shrugged and sipped my coffee.

"I have no idea. I went to Sarah's place last night to talk to her. But we didn't do much talking."

"I don't want to know that."

"She told me she loved me," I said, looking at him to gage his reaction.

"That fits with what I initially told you about her. She has issues."

"Funny. But more importantly, if I hadn't known she was with Holt, I'd believe her. Now, I'm questioning what the hell is going on."

Pete nodded and set his coffee cup down.

"Does beg the question, why she would spend the afternoon with the man who at this moment is suspect one in her sister's disappearance."

I nodded my head. I didn't know what else to do.

"We need to talk to Webster," Pete said.

I groaned aloud. I didn't know what else to do.

# 70

We sat in Webster's office. He was looking at us, one, then the other, back and forth.

"What?" he said.

"Was Mickey Holt a suspect in the disappearance?" Pete asked.

"What have you two been smoking? Are you nuts? Holt is a major entrepreneur in this city. He has helped finance a lot of projects for the city, donating a lot of time and money."

"Part of that donating was for Diana's Garden," I said.

"Exactly. Now you ask if he could have disappeared her. You two are morons."

"I assume by your attitude the answer is no," Pete said.

"Get out of my office. Now."

We stood to leave. I paused at the door and looked back at Webster.

"Every time we come here with legit questions, you kick us out. Makes me wonder what you're hiding."

"With questions like you're asking, it makes me wonder how you ever get a client. And don't accuse me of something you can't back up, asshole."

We walked out of the station. I was mad. Pete was smiling.

"What's so funny?"

"You accuse Webster of hiding something. Strikes me as funny."

"Why?"

"The way you left the force and how he holds it against you. I don't know, it's funny to me."

"Can you get hold of yourself long enough to come up with a plan?"

"Go see Ben Collier."

"That's your plan?"

We got into Pete's car and headed to the Big Beach area, both silent as we rode. It irked me that Pete was right about me accusing Webster of anything. I had no reason to cast any pebbles, much less stones.

As we approached the Collier house, Pete slowed down.

"Don't stop. Keep going. Go."

He sped up a little and drove past the house.

"Why?"

"That car is Sarah's car. Pull up somewhere and let's watch."

As Pete found a spot to park, I was thinking about what Sarah could be doing here. It was her parents' house, but I suspected everything. Maybe she knew Holt was a suspect too and was trying to get information from her father.

Pete parked the car, and we waited. When Sarah came from the house, she was mad. She walked toward her car in the driveway, her father following behind, trying to talk to her. She threw her hand up in the universal sign of screw you.

We waited a little longer.

# 71

Ben Collier stared at us when he opened the door. His face grew agitated, then angry as he recognized Pete and me.

"What now?"

Pete and I had decided in the car not to be so polite. To push and accuse and be abrasive if need be. This seemed like a good time to be that way.

"We think Mickey Holt killed your daughter," I said, watching his face for a reaction.

His brow furrowed. He held his head down to look at the ground. He looked back at me.

"Are you sleeping with my daughter?"

I just stared at him. He was watching me for a reaction. I hoped I didn't give him one.

"One of you are. Since Mr. Connolly here is a little too old for Sarah, I must assume it is you, Langley."

It wasn't lost on me it was Mr. Connolly for Pete and just Langley for me.

Pete intervened before I could respond.

"You can dodge the question, but we will just keep asking."

Collier looked at Pete.

"I didn't hear a question. I heard a ludicrous statement made by a ridiculous man."

"We are just trying to find out what happened to Diana. Seems after all this time, you'd want to know the truth."

"Mr. Connolly, I assure you the truth of Diana's disappearance is known. She was kidnapped and never seen again. I have done my best to move on and raise the family I had left. But Sarah's constant picking at old wounds makes it hard to live in the present. Good day."

He closed the door on us. As we walked back to the car, I thought maybe he was right.

I didn't like the man, but I couldn't let that stand in the way of what he had just said. Sarah had been picking at this case for decades. It had to hurt each time nothing came of it.

Collier and Holt were, if not friends, then business partners. We got in the car and as Pete backed out, I said,

"I wonder how involved Collier is with Mickey Holt."

Pete put the car in drive, then looked at me.

"That's a good question. I'd like to know if he has any connection to Island Housing. He's not on any of the paperwork with the state."

"Sounds like a job for Barbara and Kim."

"Maybe Kim. Barbara is busy in court today."

Pete took his cell phone from his pocket and handed it to me. I dialed Kim's number and told her what I wanted to know.

# 72

Pete dropped me at my truck at his house, and I went to the Clover Leaf. I needed to drink and forget this case for a little while.

The bar was empty when I came in. The houselights were on. The bar was bright. Amanda looked up at me as I walked toward my seat at the bar.

"Jesus, Joe. I haven't even opened my register yet."

"It's all right. You don't need a register to run a tab, do you?"

"You need to pay your tab. This isn't a charity, you know. You pay your tab the owner might be able to afford that European vacation he talks about."

She set my drink in front of me along with a cocktail napkin.

"Europe is overrated," I said, winking at her. She shook her head and moved on about her work. I watched her. It was one of my favorite hobbies. She flipped me the bird when she caught me staring at her ass. I smiled.

In a moment, she came walking over to me from behind the bar. She set a fresh drink down, picked up my old glass.

"Can I tell you something?" she said.

"If you want to run away together, I can be ready in ten minutes, give or take," I said.

She frowned. And for a moment, I cursed myself for flirting with her, even if it was a half ass attempt. She put up with crap like that every day in this job. I didn't want to be just another jerk in a bar.

"You can tell me anything you want," I said, as I sipped my drink.

She placed her elbows on the bar, leaning in.

"That girl you're in here with, the one that I guess hired you that night? Remember when you got beat up that night outside?"

I remembered. How could I forget? I nodded again.

"I talked to the other bartenders here, and no one remembers hearing you got attacked until I told them. They sure didn't tell her you got attacked."

"What?"

"No one in here knew you were beat up outside to tell that to her. You'd said she told you one of us told her. How would they tell her, anyway?"

She stood from leaning on the bar. She touched my hand and said,

"You're one of my all-time favorite people who come in here, Joe. But what have you gotten in to?"

I sipped my drink, wondering the same thing.

# 73

I used the phone at the bar to call Kim. I wanted to know what she had found out. When she answered the phone, she wasted no time on formality.

"How drunk are you?"

"Whatever happened to hello?"

Silence. I said,

"Wanted to know what you found on their connections."

"We've looked into that earlier. And we found nothing other than the park. Until Island Housing. I found Collier's signature on a few documents at the tax office."

"What documents?"

"Property transfers mostly. Property moving from sellers to Collier, then to Island Housing. For instance, the park started out owned by the city, then transferred to Collier, then to Island Housing. Other property is the same way."

"Rita Franklin's house?"

"Yep. That was the last property transferred in such a way. That was years ago."

I thanked her and hung up the phone. I looked at Amanda. She was shelving bottles.

"I may be back tonight," I said.

"I'll be here."

I left the bar, not sure what my next move was. I had a lot of information, but none of it seemed to fit.

Mickey Holt was the only suspect. His actions had been enough to make one wonder about his involvement.

I walked to my apartment. When I got inside, I called Sarah. She answered on the third ring.

"What are you doing tonight?" I said.

"You maybe."

I could hear her smile over the phone.

"Can you come over?" I asked.

"I'll be there in a few."

She hung up. I held onto the receiver, not sure I wanted to follow the path my gut was telling me to take.

Tonight would not be a night of lovemaking, if I could resist her, anyway. It would be a night of tough questions and serious answers.

I made a pot of coffee to counteract the booze I'd had earlier. I needed to a clear head and to be alert.

Sarah had some questions to answer. I wanted to know more about her father and Mickey Holt. I would get those answers tonight.

I poured a cup of coffee and waited for Sarah to arrive.

# 74

After two hours, I got nervous. Sarah hadn't arrived, and she hadn't answered my phone calls.

I knew there were still dangerous people out there that were hurting anyone involved in this case. I got my gun from the bedside table, checked the loads, and stuffed it into my waistband in the back.

I headed out the door. I went to my truck, placed the gun in the door pocket, and headed to Sarah's apartment.

She didn't answer. I could hear no movement from inside. I didn't have a key. I gave the door a good kick. It held solid. I kicked again.

The jamb splintered, and the door flew inward. I searched the place. She wasn't home.

I called Pete. He was closer to the Colliers than I was right now. And he hadn't been drinking. Though I felt sober as a preacher now.

He agreed to check her parents' house, then meet at the Clover Leaf. On the way to the bar, I stopped at my place to see if she was there. It was empty.

I headed to the Clover Leaf to wait for Pete. There were several people in the bar, but not too many. It was just now getting dark. The crowd would arrive soon. I took a seat at a table to wait. Amanda came over to ask if I was all right.

I asked for coffee. She nodded and brought it to me.

Thirty minutes later, Pete, Kim, and Barbara came into the bar. It was the first time I ever remembered Kim coming into the Clover Leaf. They came to my table and sat down.

"Figured we needed reinforcements in case something happened to her," Pete said, nodding at the women.

"You need to hear this," I said, motioning to Amanda.

I told Amanda to pull up a chair and at my urging she repeated what she'd told me earlier that evening about my attack and how no one knew.

"So, she lied," Kim said.

"That's two lies I caught her in. Seeing her dad that day and now this. Both are innocent if taken by themselves. Put them together..."

"Makes you wonder who she's covering for," Pete said.

"Sounds like you need a police officer. I can call my dad. He's a cop," Amanda said.

I looked at her.

"I didn't know your dad was a cop," I said.

"Oh, yeah, he's one of the good guys. Captain James Webster."

I sat and stared at her. I realized how much I didn't know about a woman I talked to every day.

Pete laughed. Kim shook her head. Barbara looked confused.

"We need to hope nothing happened to her. There are still some dangerous people out there," Pete said.

I couldn't disagree.

# 75

We left the Clover Leaf. I rode with Kim as Pete and Barbara rode in his car. We split up, looking everywhere we knew to look. Me and Kim went to Rita Franklin's house to see if Sarah's car was there. It wasn't.

Then to Astrid Franklin's apartment. I didn't know if Astrid was out of the hospital yet, but Sarah's car was nowhere to be seen.

Pete and Barbara were going to Mickey Holt's house. Kim pulled to the curb and sat idling and tapping the steering wheel with one finger.

"Where could she be?" Kim asked.

I didn't know. I had no answers. I had a fear in the pit of my stomach nagging me. I tried to voice it, but words didn't come. I tried again.

"What if whoever attacked you has her? The same man who killed Rita Franklin."

Kim looked to her left, then said,

"I know you care for her, but we don't know that."

"We don't know anything. That's the problem."

"Well, we have to do something."

Kim's cell phone rang. She answered it, listened, then fumbled in the middle console for a pen and paper. She wrote a number down, then pushed the end button.

"Call this number. Sarah called Pete, needing to talk to you."

She handed me the paper and her phone. I looked at the number.

"This isn't Sarah's number."

Kim shrugged as if to say, what do you want me to do?

I punched the number into the phone and listened as it finally connected and began ringing.

Sarah answered on the second ring.

"Sarah? Are you OK? Where are you? I'll come get you."

"Joe, stop. Listen to me, OK."

I could hear in her voice she had been crying. I wanted to reach through the phone and hold her.

"What's wrong?"

She sniffled.

"Will you really come get me?"

"Of course, I would. Tell me where you are." "I made a mistake, Joe."

She didn't answer my questions. She just kept talking as if I had said nothing. I needed to keep her talking.

"What kind of mistake?"

She cried into the phone.

"Remember when I said I love you? You never said anything back."

I glanced over at Kim, who was watching me.

"Of course, I love you, Sarah. Is that the mistake you're talking about?"

"No, Joe. I do love you. The mistake was blaming Ralph Norris all these years when he had nothing to do with Diana's death."

Her words startled me. She was admitting she was wrong.

"You were operating on emotions, not facts, Sarah. Let me come get you."

"You're so sweet, Joe. I need you. Come get me."

The phone went dead. I screamed her name into the phone. Kim grabbed the phone from me.

"That's not helping."

She pressed redial. The call went to voicemail. She tried two more times. Same result.

The phone rang in her hands. I looked at the screen. The ID said Peter C.

Kim answered it, holding a finger up at me.

# 76

Kim held the phone out to me again. I took it and instantly started talking.

"Pete, they, someone has Sarah. I don't know where she is, but she was a crying mess and..."

"Joe, listen. I called Webster before I called you guys the first time. He ran a trace on the number while you talked. They triangulated it back to Big Beach."

"Her parents' house?" I said.

"Maybe. She wasn't there earlier. Maybe she is now. We are heading that way. So is Webster."

"We're on our way," I said, disconnecting the call.

I told Kim where to go. She drove faster than I would have, but I was glad for it. What was her father doing to Sarah to make her cry like that? The hatred I felt for that man was immense. What was the reason for it? I shook my head. I didn't need a reason. We needed to hurry.

"Go faster, please."

Kim looked at me as if she wanted to slap me. I rode the rest of the way silently.

I couldn't help but be afraid for Sarah. My gun was still in my truck at the Clover Leaf. That was a good thing because if her father had hurt her, I'd bury that man. I knew that.

Kim and I arrived at almost the same time Pete and Barbara did. We both pulled up to Collier's house and got out, the women waiting in the car.

As Pete and I ran up the yard, I grabbed his arm and slowed him down. I pointed to a car in the driveway.

"Holt's here," Pete said.

I nodded.

"Whatever they are doing to her in there, I'm going to kill them both," I said.

We ran up on the porch. Pete looked as if he were about to knock. I ran past him at full force. I slammed my shoulder into the door.

It broke the jamb, the molding on the wall flying off in pieces. The glass in the door shattered from the force, sending shards flying into the entryway.

From the living room area, Collier and Holt came running to see what had happened. Marie Collier stood behind them, her hand to her mouth. "What is the meaning of this?" he said, staring at us.

"Have you two lost your minds?" Mickey asked, looking as disheveled as always.

"Where is she?" I said, stepping toward Collier.

He must have known he was in danger because he stepped back and held up his hands.

"Who? What are you talking about?"

Mickey stepped between me and Collier. Pushing him away, I pointed a finger at him.

"I know what you did, you bastard. Where is Sarah?"

"Nobody in this house knows what you are talking about," Holt said.

"Sarah is missing," Pete said, taking my arm in hand and pulling me back. "If you don't want me to release him to do what he wants to do so badly, you best tell us where she is."

Flashing red and blue lights cut off whatever Collier was going to say. Webster came into the house and looked the scene over. He got in front of me, his face an inch from mine, and said,

"Get your ass outside before I arrest you."

Pete pulled me out of the house and into the yard. I waited for Webster and whatever he would do.

# 77

Kim and Barbara had joined Pete and me in the yard. I could hear loud voices coming from the house but couldn't make out what they said. Webster came out to stand next to us.

He looked at me and Pete, his thumbs in his belt loop of his slacks.

"First, they are pissed at you two for breaking into their house."

"I don't care about that. Sarah is missing and you know she is," I said.

He held a hand up, palm out, and said,

"Second, they don't know where she is."

I looked from Pete to Webster. I couldn't hold my anger in any longer.

"You said the phone call was traced back to this area."

Webster nodded.

"I did. But she isn't here. Her father said they were supposed to meet for dinner tonight. All of them," he said, jerking his head back toward the house. "But she hasn't shown yet."

Pete shook his head, then said,

"That makes no sense, Captain. That phone call was tracked back..."

"Pete," I said, interrupting. "She ain't here."

He gave me a strange look. I said,

"She knows Mickey Holt is the main suspect. I told her that much. This was all a ploy to get everyone in the same place."

"It failed. She isn't here," Pete said.

"Not here. Diana's Garden. That's where she is." "If Holt is in danger, I have to warn him," Webster said, walking back to the house.

In a few minutes, we all left the house and, in separate cars, drove to the little park a few blocks from the Collier house.

When Kim pulled up to the park, the headlights of her car shined toward the fountain. My heart leapt at what I saw.

Sarah sat on the lip of the fountain, her legs dangling. She wasn't looking anywhere but toward the ground.

As Kim parked, I got out of the car and walked toward Sarah. I could hear the others behind me as they parked their cars.

"Sarah. Are you all right?"

She looked up at me, the car headlights reflecting the tears in her eyes.

"Joe. I'm so glad you came. Is everyone else here?"

"What's wrong? What do you mean?"

Ronnie Ashmore

"I know the truth." she said, smiling at me.

# 78

The look she gave me while smiling scared me. It was the look of a person who had reached the breaking point. Like they couldn't suffer any more pain or heartbreak. I couldn't tell if she had been drinking or not.

"I think I figured the truth too," I said.

She shook her head and looked up to face the sky. She laughed, then said,

"I wasted so many years doing this. Hurting people."

I stood a few feet from her. Different emotions flooded over me. I didn't want to approach her, but I wanted to protect her at the same time.

Webster, Ben Collier, and Mickey Holt came up to stand on my left. Pete, Barbara, and Kim stood on my right. I stared at Sarah, searching for what to say.

Her father spoke first.

"What is the meaning of this, Sarah? We were supposed to have dinner tonight."

"I'm not hungry," she said, as if she were a child refusing to eat her vegetables.

"What are you doing here?" Ben asked.

Sarah shrugged her shoulders, holding the position for a moment before relaxing them.

"I'm visiting my sister's garden."

"Well," Ben said, throwing his hands up. "This is foolishness."

Webster leaned in toward me. He said,

"Foolish or not, I have a crisis team coming."

I nodded. To Sarah I said,

"I know for a long time you suspected your neighbor. You were misled, though."

She looked at me.

"Ralph Norris. You need to say his name. I put him through hell."

"Not your fault," I said. "The people you hired misled you."

"You weren't fooled or misled. You stayed the course no matter what. I wasted all my money and all those years, when I should have just hired a drunk P.I. and been done."

I looked over at Kim and Pete. They shook their heads in unison. I didn't know what to do next.

She shifted her seat on the fountain. She began kicking her legs out as if she were a little girl sitting on a porch railing.

Beside me, Mickey Holt shifted from foot to foot. He said,

"This is ridiculous. I'm going home."

Sarah lifted her shirt tail, wiping her eyes and nose.

"You can't go yet, Mr. Holt. We are just getting started," she said.

Holt huffed beside me. In the distance, a siren wailed. A minute later, an ambulance pulled up and two EMTs got out and walked up to us.

# 79

The two EMTs walked up to where we all stood. Webster said,

"I don't know what we have yet. She's in distress but I want her to keep talking. You guys stand by."

At the same time, Holt looked at Ben, who stood staring at his daughter. He said,

"Ben, get control of your daughter. She is crazy. She needs help."

Collier ignored his friend. I didn't think she had a weapon, but I wasn't sure. She could have a knife or something just as deadly. I wanted to keep her talking.

Not knowing what else to say, I said,

"Sarah?"

She looked at me. She smiled again.

"You said you knew the truth when I spoke to you on the phone. What is that truth, baby?"

"Baby?" she said, staring at me. "Do you love me, Joe? I love you. You know?"

I could feel tears burning in my eyes. I fought to not let them fall. Kim touched my arm, showing support. That made my eyes burn more.

From beside me, Pete said,

"Sarah. You were going to tell us what you figured out. The truth you mentioned. And why we are here."

"Pete, you are such a class act. You are expensive, too. Mother told me you cost a fortune, but you didn't figure any of this out until you teamed up with Joe."

Sarah looked at me again, then said to no one in particular,

"I am here to visit my sister."

"Sarah, you said that already," Webster said. "Let us get you some help and make you feel better."

That was typical cop speak to try to end a situation. Sarah didn't seem to hear.

She stopped talking. She turned her head to stare into the fountain. Ben Collier and Mickey Holt talked over one another to Webster, trying to bring this to an end.

Webster listened for a moment, then held up a hand to silence them.

"You both be quiet. And stay here. I may need you later."

I watched Sarah. Thinking about our time together. The lovemaking, the laughter, the drunken nights. Our conversations always turned to her missing sister. I thought of all these things watching this beautiful woman sitting on the fountain's edge staring at the water.

The pieces all fell into place.

"My God, Sarah?"

She looked up at me. She nodded her head. I felt my stomach sink. Or was that what a heartbreaking felt like. Either way, I hated the feeling.

# 80

Sarah was looking at me, shaking her head, struggling to find the words to speak. Beside me, I could see the others from my peripheral staring at me.

"I was hoping this would be like the other times," Sarah said.

"What's that mean?" Webster asked.

"I'm talking to Joe now," she said.

Webster swore under his breath. Collier and Holt were standing still, watching Sarah.

"You figured it out, didn't you?" she asked. I nodded my head. Slowly. I looked over at Mickey Holt. He was looking at the ground, looking as disheveled as ever. His polo shirt torn and ripped in places. His jeans seemed to not fit him right.

"Don't look at him, Joe. Look at me. Tell me what you figured out."

"You have known all this time that Diana is dead. You kept the ruse of looking into the disappearance so you could lead someone to the truth of Mickey Holt being responsible."

She laughed a loud laugh. She slid off the lip of the fountain. She stood on the ground, looking at me.

"So close, Joe. You missed it like everyone else. Not just Mickey Holt. Good ol' Uncle Mickey," she said, staring at Holt.

Holt looked up when she mentioned his name. His face looked ashen, and in the darkness, lit only by headlights and the flashing red and blue strobes of the ambulance, he looked on the verge of hysteria.

"Captain Webster! I demand you take custody of this woman and get her the mental help she needs," Holt said.

"You have no say in her medical condition, Holt. Stand still."

"I do have say, Captain," Ben Collier said. "I agree with Mickey. Do something."

I held up a hand to quieten them all. I was watching Sarah. She was staring at Holt and her father.

I thought I realized why she had said I was so close. I had missed an important part of the case. I thought Mickey Holt was solely to blame, but what about Ben Collier?

"Did Mickey kill your sister and your dad knew and covered it up?" I asked. "Is that why yours and his relationship is so strained? Why you two argue a lot?"

She shook her head and pointed at the two men.

"You're wrong about them. Mostly."

I took a step forward. I wanted to take her in my arms and hold her until this episode passed. It was too late for that.

"What did I miss?"

"Mickey Holt didn't kill Diana. I did."

Sarah's words hung in the air for a moment, then dropped like a bomb between us.

# 81

Mickey Holt cussed loudly. Ben Collier punched Mickey on the arm to silence him. Collier looked as if he were going to be sick.

I looked at Pete and Webster. Webster nodded and motioned for me to keep her talking. Kim touched my arm again. I pushed it away. I took a step toward Sarah.

"What do you mean?" I asked.

"I played this game for so long," she said. "I would hire a P.I. then manipulate the investigation to look where I wanted them to look. Usually to Norris. They would spend a few months and tell me there was no new evidence."

She sat in the dirt in front of the fountain and folded her knees to her chest. She looked only at me and said,

"It was my way of finding out what was known. It worked so well for so long. I couldn't manipulate you and Peter, though. Alone, I could have. I could mislead Peter and sleep with you. I used sex to control you, Joe. Until it got complicated."

I looked at the people standing around me. No one was looking at me. All eyes were on Sarah. It embarrassed me to be taken advantage of so easily.

"I do love you, Sarah."

I felt foolish saying those words now. She smiled and shook her head at me.

"You wouldn't back off. Even after being beat up. That was me and a guy I hired from my apartment building, by the way. I couldn't bring myself to kill you, Joe. But I killed Rita Franklin, beat her daughter." She looked at Kim. "I'm sorry for attacking you, Kim. You were so nice to me. But I had to, you understand?"

"All of that was you?" I asked, not believing what I was hearing.

"To protect our secret," she said, looking over at her father and Mickey Holt. "I protected it many years, dad. I hope you know that."

"Tell me the secret, Sarah," I said.

She looked at me as if she were thinking about it, then nodded her head.

"Diana isn't missing. She's under this fountain. That's where the three of us put her."

I looked over at Collier. Tears glistened on his cheeks. I turned back to Sarah.

"Three of you? Holt, your dad, and you?"

"She was always at the basketball court that was here then. Shooting hoops. Acting like a spoiled brat all the time, like she was dad's favorite. He sent me to get her one evening. She refused to come home. Told me dad would be OK with her staying. We argued. I hit her, a stupid fight. But then I had my hands around her neck, squeezing. Then she was..."

Her voice trailed off. She was silent for a long time. I was speechless. I had no words for what I had just heard. Pete broke the silence.

"What happened then?"

Sarah looked at him. She said,

"I went home crying. Dad asked what was wrong. I told him I hurt Diana. He came running down here. Then Uncle Mickey was here somehow. They hid her somewhere. I don't know that part. But a month or so later, when this fountain was being poured. We buried her underneath it. They covered her with concrete and the rest..."

# 82

She stopped talking. Webster moved over to Collier. He pulled handcuffs from his pocket and locked Ben Collier's wrist in them. Ben protested.

"Shut the hell up, Collier. You're under arrest," Webster said, locking the cuffs in place.

He looked at Holt as he reached into his pocket for another set of cuffs.

"Mickey Holt, you're under arrest, too."

He locked the cuffs on Holt, who stood there in silence. Not looking up.

I went to Sarah. Taking her hands, I helped her to her feet. She was crying hard now. I hugged her close to me, stroking her hair.

"You poor woman. Living with this guilt your whole life."

I could feel her tears on my shoulder as her body shaking as she sobbed.

"I didn't mean to...I never meant to hurt her...She was such a brat..."

I stepped back and broke our embrace.

"You've hurt a lot of people, Sarah."

"I know."

She wiped her hand over her face, snot and tears mixed in a long string from her nose to her hand.

"I never meant to. It's your fault, damnit."

"My fault? How?"

She looked into my eyes.

"You wouldn't back off. You and Peter kept pushing. I beat you up. I burned his office down. I killed...I don't even want to think about all I have done. Yet, you kept pushing."

I stepped back farther. I looked over to where the others were standing. Webster had seated Ben Collier and Mickey Holt on the ground, one on each side of his front bumper. Pete stood between them, making sure they didn't talk to each other.

Kim and Barbara were looking at me. Webster walked toward me. His hands were empty. I turned back and faced Sarah.

"A lot of people were hurt over all these years. But I damn sure had nothing to do with it. You're the killer, Sarah. Not me."

"We will be OK, though, Joe. Right? It will be OK. I love you. You said you love me, too."

Webster placed a hand on Sarah's arm. He guided her toward his car. Two more patrol units showed up as he walked her toward the cars.

I walked beside him. To Sarah, he said,

"You're going to have to tell all this again at the station. Officially."

"OK." she said. "Then Joe can take me home, right?"

"You'll be going to jail for a long time, Sarah," I said.

She stopped walking and looked at me.

"You'll visit though, won't you?"

I shook my head. Something turned over inside me, making me feel sick.

"I don't visit people in prison."

Webster led her off to one of the patrol units. I watched as they put the handcuffs on her wrists. Her tears seemed to be cried out. She was staring off in the distance.

Pete came to stand beside me. Sarah looked over at us as the officer placed her in the car. I thought she smiled at me.

"So much destruction. I'm sorry Joe. I know you cared for her," Pete said.

I only stared toward the patrol car, imagining I could see her inside the dark interior.

"I'll see you later. I need a drink."

I walked off into the darkness. I was a long way from the Clover Leaf, but right now that was what I needed. A drink, and some quiet time to think about all I had found and lost.

# ABOUT THE AUTHOR

Ronnie Ashmore writes westerns and crime novels. His books make you feel you are eavesdropping on real people because he has an ability to give his characters an authentic voice and a sense of reality.

When he is not working or writing and has some spare time, he enjoys playing golf, fishing, and traveling.

He would love to hear from you. You can contact him at ronnieashmorebooks@gmail.com

# ABOUT THE PUBLISHER

Creative Texts is a boutique independent publishing house devoted to high quality content that readers enjoy. We publish best-selling authors such as Ronnie Ashmore, Jerry D. Young, N.C. Reed, Sean Liscom, Jared McVay, Laurence Dahners, and many more. Our audiobook performers are among the best in the business including Hollywood legends like Barry Corbin and top talent like Christopher Lane, Alyssa Bresnaham, Erin Moon and Graham Hallstead.

Whether its post-apocalyptic or dystopian fiction, biography, history, true crime science fiction, thrillers, or even classic westerns, our goal is to produce highly rated customer preferred content. If there is anything we can do to enhance your reader experience, please contact us directly at info@creativetexts.com. As always, we do appreciate your reviews on your book seller's website.

Finally, if you would like to find more great books like this one, please search for us by name in your favorite search engine or on your bookseller's website to see books by all Creative Texts authors.

Thank you for reading!

# MORE FROM RONNIE ASHMORE

**Colby PD Series**
Family Secrets
Colby Nights

**John Riley Bounty Hunter Series**
The Losing Trail
The Killing Trail
The Vengeance Trail
The Deceiving Trail
A Bullet for Malo
The Claren Range Dispute

**Sam Bolton Ex Ranger**
Duty Bound
Fighting Men
Crooked Trail

**Other Books**
Last Stand for a Bad Man
Texas: 1857

**Non-Fiction**
Lessons on Leadership:
Leading Behind the Badge

**Jim Long**
Homecoming
Lawman